DINOTOPIA®
THE WORLD BENEATH

DINOTOPIA: THE WORLD BENEATH

Written and Illustrated by James Gurney

HarperCollinsPUBLISHERS

FOR JEANETTE

Among many who have generously assisted with their insight and expertise,
I would like to thank: Michael Brett-Surman, Ken Carpenter, Ralph Chapman,
Rodolfo Coria, Linda Deck, Alan Foster, Timothy Kendall, Jim Kirkland, and
Mike Williams. In memory of Ian Ballantine, whose spirit and whose name
gave life to Enit and Nallab.

The second in a series of Dinotopia® books.

Originally published by Turner Publishing, Inc.

Dinotopia® is a registered trademark of BDSP, Inc.

Dinotopia: *The World Beneath*
Copyright © 1995 by James Gurney. Licensed by the Beanstalk Group.

Library of Congress Cataloging-in-Publication Data
Gurney, James, 1958–
  Dinotopia : the World Beneath / written and illustrated by James Gurney.
    p.   cm.
  Sequel to Dinotopia : a land apart from time.
  Summary: Four years after being shipwrecked on the lost island of Dinotopia, sixteen-year-old
Will Denison, now a fully trained Skybax Corps pilot, explores the skies over the island while his
scientist father leads an expedition into the forgotten caverns of the legendary World Beneath.
  ISBN 0-06-028006-9 — ISBN 0-06-053065-0 (pbk.)
  [1. Fantasy.   2. Dinosaurs—Fiction.   3. Islands—Fiction.   4. Adventure and adventurers—
Fiction.]   I. Title.
PZ7.G98158Di   1998   98-5574
[Fic]—dc21   CIP
                                                                        AC

❖
www.harperchildrens.com
www.dinotopia.com

"Here on Dinotopia my eyes have been opened to the wonders of a new world."

So wrote naturalist Arthur Denison as he completed the first volume of his journals on the island of Dinotopia, the land where people and dinosaurs live in peaceful interdependence.

He and his son, Will, had been shipwrecked there in 1862. During their first four years on the island, Will passed the tests that allowed him to ride on the largest flying creature that ever lived, the skybax.

Arthur's boundless curiosity drew him not up to the sky, but rather deep into the earth. He became one of the first in recent times to journey into the forgotten caverns of the World Beneath—and return to tell the tale. What he found there, and what he was yet to find, came to be known as the Denison Expedition, a chapter of wonder and danger in the history of the land apart from time.

THE COOL MIST clung to Waterfall City on the morning of March 12, 1867, covering each person and each dinosaur with a fine nimbus of sparkling droplets. At the first bloom of light, well-wishers encouraged Will Denison, the humans saying "Fly high," or "Be bold." The dinosaurs rumbled affectionately. Will stepped out on the flight platform where his father's experimental aircraft awaited its first flight. He shook away the droplets from his hair and wiped his forehead with his sleeve.

The Dragoncopter is
ready for its first flight
over Waterfall City

Designed after a dragonfly

Two sets of flapping wings

The steam engine gives only five minutes' flying time

Arthur Denison checked the steam pressure in the boiler. "Pressure, ready. Throttle, ready. Elevator, ready," he said. "This is it, Will. Remember, you're not on a skybax. *You* are in charge of the flying. And the engine will give you only five minutes of power before you have to glide."

"Don't worry, Father," replied Will. "I trained on gliders in Canyon City."

Arthur cautions his son

The Dragoncopter loses altitude

Bix, the translator-*Protoceratops*, turned to Will's skybax, Cirrus. "Please fly close beside Will," she squawked. "He is sixteen summers old, a reckless age for humans."

The moment of truth had arrived. Arthur opened a valve and spun the flywheel. The engine sputtered a rhythm: chuff, chuff, chuff, chuff. Will pushed forward on the control handles. The wings raised and lowered, then fluttered like a moth, lifting the Dragoncopter away from its platform.

Bix advises Cirrus to fly close by in case of danger

"Pull up! Pull up!"

At first the flying machine dipped low, then struggled upward, skimming over the tile rooftops. The smell of the kerosene and the noise of the engine exhilarated Will. He circled the One-Earth Globe and shot out above Cloudbottom Gorge.

Suddenly something lurched in the engine. One wing stopped moving; the other three still wobbled up and down. The five-minute timer had almost run out. Will pulled back on the control handles. No response. He looked up. Ahead of him was a deadly white curtain of thundering water!

The Dragoncopter dives toward Lower Thunder Falls

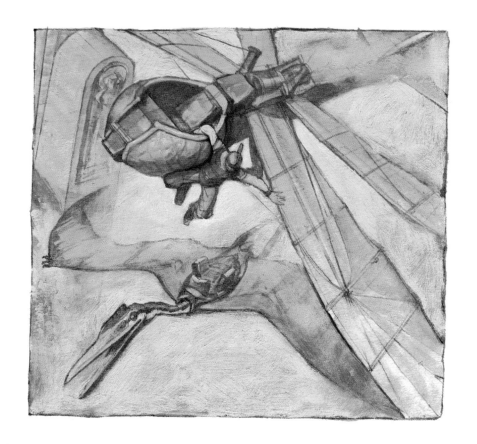

Will saw that Cirrus, at great risk, had flown just below him, providing his only chance for survival. Lifting himself out of the cockpit, he braced himself until the saddle appeared right under his feet. Then he jumped, grabbing hold just as the skybax swerved to keep its wing tip free of the thundering water. The Dragoncopter buried its head in the foam and was instantly dragged down, never to be seen again.

Returning safely to the platform, Will felt grateful to be alive. He had never been so glad to feel solid stone under his feet, nor so happy to greet his fellow living creatures.

*Last-minute leap
to the skybax saddle*

Crash and rescue

"My father is not going to be too happy about my losing the Dragoncopter," said Will. "He built it himself. How can I replace it?"

"That would be easy," said Bix. "Replacing *you* would be impossible. You are a very good skybax rider, and we can't spare you."

"Thanks, Bix. My father has plans for me, too. He says that someday I'll operate flying machines that will go faster and higher than any skybax."

"I'm glad he believes in you," said Bix. "He has good reason to. But he might be putting too much faith in machines. Wonderful as they are, they have no judgment of their own. No heart, no sense, no love for you. Stay with your skybax. Flying machines will never take over the skies."

Arthur appeared on the platform looking shaken. "Will, thank heaven you're safe," he said. "Let's find a ride over to my laboratory."

Will returns with Arthur to the laboratory

THE THICK WALLS of Arthur Denison's laboratory muffled the distant rumble of the waters.

"Why did you have to be a daredevil?" said Arthur. "You risked your life and lost my ship."

"You didn't tell me the wings were going to jam," Will protested.

"It was not made for stunts."

"Why don't *you* try flying the next one?"

"Perhaps one day I will," said Arthur. "We all will. I hope to see the day when people can travel freely, not only throughout this island, but also across the ocean to the rest of the world."

"How would that be possible? No steamship or powered glider could get past the reefs and storms."

"Steam is not the answer," Arthur replied. He unlocked a drawer and lifted out a transparent stone, shaped in a six-sided pyramid. "Dinotopia may be more advanced than it appears. There's more than meets the eye. When I made my short trip through the caves beneath this island, I found this stone. It seems to have been recut from its natural crystalline form, but I can't scratch it or chip it, even with a diamond. Look how it glows. It stores and transmits the energy of the sun and refracts light in a reverse spectrum, quite the opposite of the normal laws of physics."

"Is it magic?"

"No, I believe it is science, but an ancient, strange science, quite unknown in Europe or America."

"Where is this science now?"

"Lost. Forgotten," said Arthur. "Or hidden."

Arthur shows Will the mysterious stone

Artifacts from the World Beneath

Gold cup shows an athlete ready to jump over Triceratops

Statuette of kneeling Allosaurus figure with double spiral

Inlaid pendant of Quetzalcoatlus

front

back

Protective amulet of Stegosaurus in defensive posture

Clay portrait of Triceratops with human features

Arthur brought out more artifacts. They gleamed in the light as Will turned them in his hand. "Who made these?" asked Will.

"I don't know. I found them near a sealed door. Beyond that door is surely the answer to the mystery of this stone and its powers. I've got to get back down there."

"But you and Bix barely made it out alive."

Just then a puff of cigar smoke drifted into the room. "You don't know the highways and byways on this island like I do, Professor. You need my know-how to get back into those caves."

"Lee Crabb. What are you doing here?" demanded Arthur.

Crabb grinned. "A good hand knows when he'll be needed. I just happened to hear your jawtackle about the ancient science. I've learned a thing or two about it myself. And what I've learned you can't find in a library."

"What do you have in mind?" asked Arthur.

"I'm an adventuring man, and I'm handy in a squall. I've got the kind of sub you'll need, and I know all about the sunken entrance. I can get you in there. But many a blighter has gone in and not come out. Old Lee can get you out. Or, if you've a mind," he said, studying Arthur's face, "we might get each other off this brig ship of an island." With his rough hand, he patted Arthur's notebook. "Your science is worth more in Paris than in Pooktook."

"I'll think about it," said Arthur. "But first I want to find out at the Round Table meeting what the dinosaurs can tell us about the secrets of the caves."

Lee Crabb listens from the doorway

Humans require high chairs to reach the Round Table

The elders assemble to discuss the expedition

Arthur called a special meeting of the dinosaur and human elders to deliver his proposal for a new expedition. The ponderous creatures gathered around the table, humming in low tones. Some sat quietly at their places with eyes closed in meditation. Even though he had spent five years in Dinotopia, Arthur was still not entirely accustomed to regarding dinosaurs as equals. He watched the leathery giants: teachers, historians, geologists, librarians, each with their special costumes and ornaments. They reminded him of owls in an aviary—wise, alert, and dignified.

An elderly *Stegosaurus* named Almaron rattled his plates and drummed his foot on the speaking platform for attention. He reared up to his full standing height and began to speak in a wheezy voice that Bix translated for Arthur.

"As we all know, there is a land of story and song called The World Beneath. Our dear Bix, along with Professor Denison, claims to have visited this place, and they wish to go again."

There was a coughing and a shuffling of feet. A majestic *Triceratops* named Brokehorn shifted his six-ton bulk on his resting couch and said, "Let the professor have his say."

Arthur cleared his throat. "My first trip into the World Beneath was just a preliminary glimpse," he said. "I was not prepared for a long journey. The caves are extensive, with large chambers lit by a strange phosphorescence. I found clear evidence of very ancient occupation by dinosaurs alone, and later by human cultures, which left artifacts, carvings, and wall paintings."

Nallab is the assistant librarian

Enit, the head librarian, takes notes on a Pedostenograph

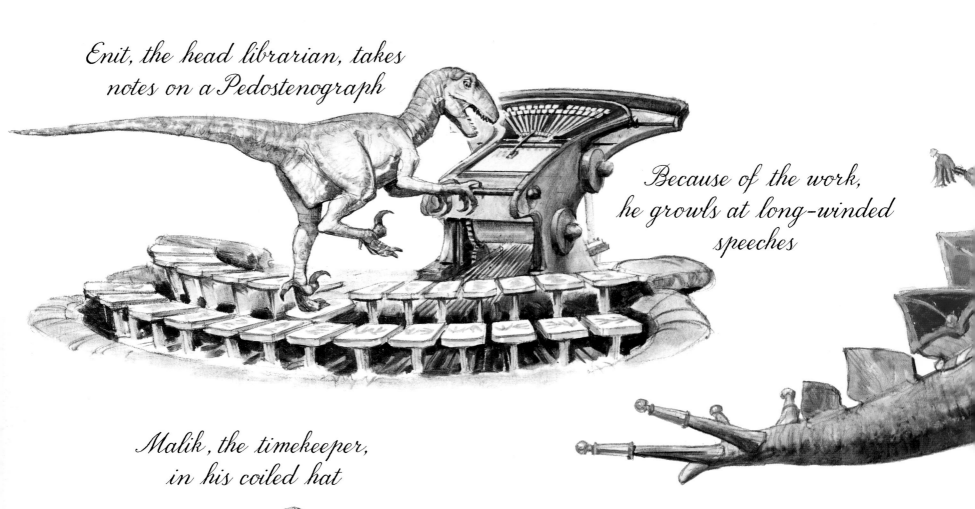

Because of the work, he growls at long-winded speeches

Malik, the timekeeper, in his coiled hat

Bix translates for most dinosaurs

A	B	C	D	E	F	G	H	I
J	K	L	M	N	O	P	Q	R
S	T	U	V	W	X	Y	Z	?
0	1	2	3	4	5	6	7	8	9

Footprint alphabet

[22]

The Stegosaurus Almaron is
a distinguished orator

He stamps his foot on the
speaking platform for attention

Nallab brings with him an
assortment of ancient scrolls

[23]

"Two objects in particular captured my interest. One was this hexagonal stone." He held it up. It pulsed with a soft light.

"A sunstone!" said Nallab. "So there *is* such a thing. The Scrolls of Poseidos tell of sunstones. Those scrolls are filed under fantasy, not fact. The story tells of a great king named Ogthar, half man, half dinosaur, who journeyed to the place deep in the earth where the sun goes to sleep at night. He reached into the sun's bed and plucked out a number of shining stones, along with a ruby-colored stone of a special power. He brought them to his beloved city of Poseidos, where they brought the very light of day to the streets of the city. Ogthar also brought back a nest of golden eggs which hatched into giant metallic creatures. These creatures wore the stones as jewels and received life from them."

"What happened to this city of Poseidos?" inquired Bix.

"The story says the sea grew angry at Ogthar for disturbing its rest with needless noise and light. In its wrath, the sea rose up and drowned the city."

"And what became of the sunstones?"

Arthur shows the key to Inspector Myops, an Amargasaurus

Brokehorn, son of Grayback the Wise

"Drat!" Nallab said. "I'm missing those scrolls. It's the curse of every librarian. All we are told is that King Ogthar rescued the stones and gave them in trust to another king, along with a great treasure."

Bix opened her beak. "Could there be any truth to this legend?"

Nallab shrugged. "Dinotopia has no half-human kings and no metal monsters and no Poseidos. But that hasn't stopped people from looking."

Brokehorn turned to Arthur. "What was the other thing that captured your interest?"

"A door," said Arthur. "An immense door." He produced something from his pocket. "I found this bronze key in the hand of a human skeleton. It *looks* like a key. But it didn't open the door."

A frill-necked *Amargasaurus* named Myops swung his head to study the key. "Humff. Not bronze. Orichalc. Not a whole key. Half a key. Other half lost. Never will find. Foomff."

"Let us help Professor Denison find the other half of his key so that he can begin his journey," proclaimed Brokehorn. "Look here first; Waterfall City is the place of lost and found."

"Foomff and fiffle. Dead and buried. Dusty, musty. No poke, no prod," snorted Myops.

Just then a ray of light slanted through the window and touched the sunstone. It flared in a glorious radiance that made each forget his words. Myops raised his head, frill extended, eyes wide, monocle dangling.

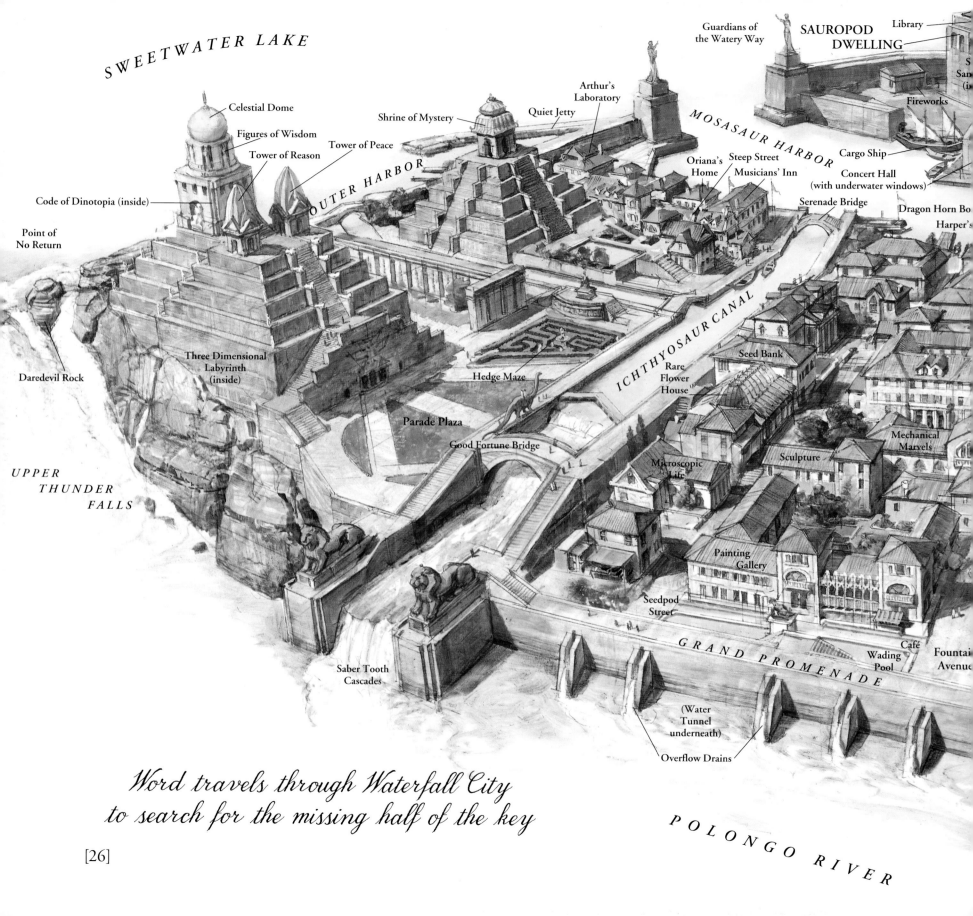

SWEETWATER LAKE

Guardians of the Watery Way

SAUROPOD DWELLING

Library

Celestial Dome

Figures of Wisdom

Arthur's Laboratory

Shrine of Mystery

Quiet Jetty

MOSASAUR HARBOR

Tower of Reason

Tower of Peace

Fireworks

Code of Dinotopia (inside)

OUTER HARBOR

Cargo Ship

Oriana's Home

Steep Street

Concert Hall (with underwater windows)

Point of No Return

Musicians' Inn

Serenade Bridge

Dragon Horn Bo

Harper's

Daredevil Rock

Three Dimensional Labyrinth (inside)

ICHTHYOSAUR CANAL

Seed Bank

Rare Flower House

Hedge Maze

UPPER THUNDER FALLS

Parade Plaza

Mechanical Marvels

Good Fortune Bridge

Microscopic Life

Sculpture

Painting Gallery

Seedpod Street

Saber Tooth Cascades

GRAND PROMENADE

Café

Wading Pool

Fountain Avenue

(Water Tunnel underneath)

Overflow Drains

*Word travels through Waterfall City
to search for the missing half of the key*

[26]

POLONGO RIVER

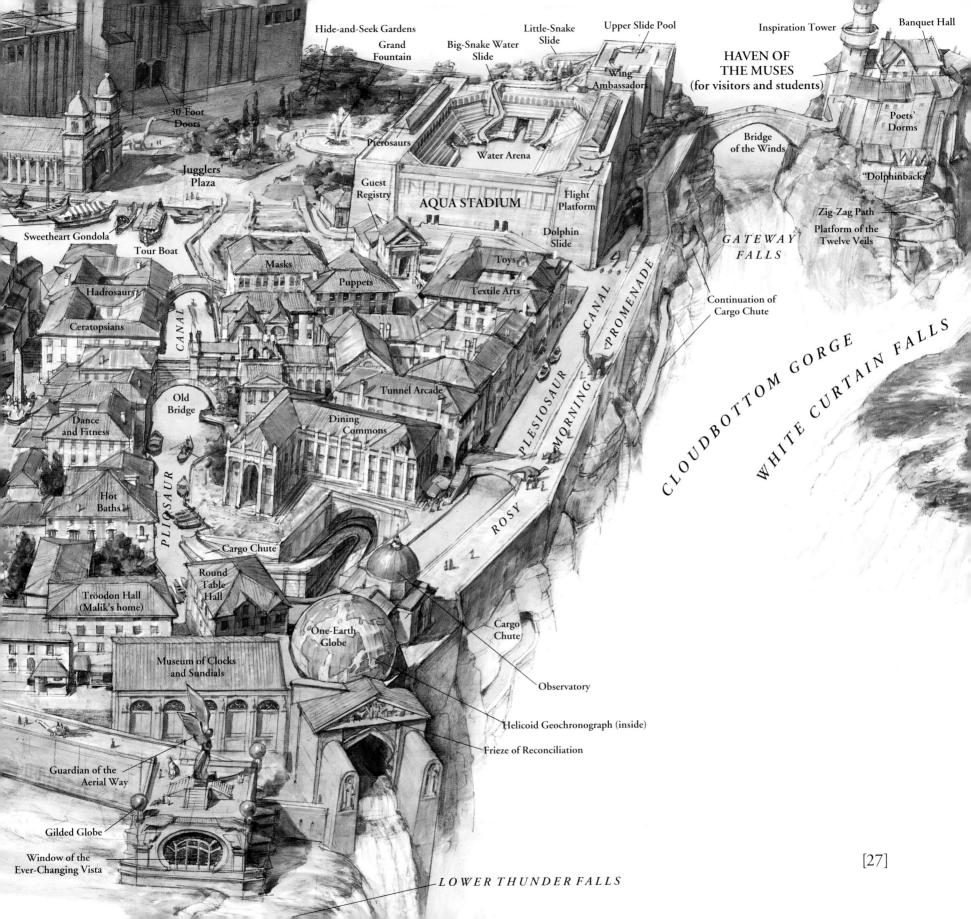

Hide-and-Seek Gardens

Grand Fountain

Big-Snake Water Slide

Little-Snake Slide

Upper Slide Pool

Inspiration Tower

Banquet Hall

HAVEN OF THE MUSES
(for visitors and students)

30-Foot Doors

Wing Ambassadors

Poets' Dorms

Pterosaurs

Water Arena

Bridge of the Winds

"Dolphinbacks"

Jugglers' Plaza

Guest Registry

AQUA STADIUM

Flight Platform

Zig-Zag Path

Platform of the Twelve Veils

Sweetheart Gondola

Dolphin Slide

GATEWAY FALLS

Tour Boat

Masks

Toys

Hadrosaurs

Puppets

Textile Arts

Continuation of Cargo Chute

CANAL

Ceratopsians

Tunnel Arcade

CLOUDBOTTOM GORGE

Old Bridge

Dining Commons

PLESIOSAUR CANAL

MORNING PROMENADE

WHITE CURTAIN FALLS

Dance and Fitness

ROSY

Hot Baths

PLIOSAUR

Cargo Chute

Tröodon Hall
(Malik's home)

Round Table Hall

One-Earth Globe

Cargo Chute

Museum of Clocks and Sundials

Observatory

Guardian of the Aerial Way

Helicoid Geochronograph (inside)

Frieze of Reconciliation

Gilded Globe

Window of the Ever-Changing Vista

LOWER THUNDER FALLS

[27]

Oriana Nascava

News about the famous key fragment reached every corner of Waterfall City by the end of that day. Trunks divulged their contents, jewelry cases hinged apart, and museum drawers opened, one after another. By sundown a line of people and dinosaurs had formed inside Round Table Hall. Each carried some odd artifact that they thought fit the description of a spiral key. There were rumors of cursed gold, of dark knowledge, and of grand rewards for the holder of the key.

A woman wearing a musician's costume stood last in line, apart from the others. She was tall and silent, her eyes riveted on Arthur's key.

"What is your name?" asked Brokehorn.

"Oriana Nascava."

"And what is your wish?"

She addressed Arthur. "Would you kindly give me, sir, the lost heirloom that is my right?" With that she produced a key that was a perfect match to Arthur's.

Waterfall City at sunset

Oriana's half

Arthur's half

*The completed
spiral key*

She continued, "This key is one of the only treasures passed down to me by my parents, who died soon after I was born. The other half was stolen from them many years before."

Arthur frowned. "But I need that key for my expedition. That is the purpose of this search."

"Very well, Professor Denison. However, it goes nowhere without me. I have a desire to join your expedition. The chain of my ancestors has been lost. My last name means 'born from a cave,' and I want to know why."

"My dear girl, I can't take *you* along. I'm afraid this is not a trip for—ah—ladies."

Bix sputtered a note of protest, prompting Oriana to say with some amusement, "Isn't Bix a lady? Didn't she save your life on your last expedition?"

Somewhat embarrassed, Arthur replied shortly, "Very well, Miss Nascava, you may come. And of course Bix will be joining me again. But to ensure the success of our trip, I'll need to find an expert guide to help us."

"Pardon me," said Lee Crabb, who stepped forward from the crowd. "But if I may say, in my humble way, given the chance, I'd be glad to have the ladies aboard. Ladies do pretty up the picture. I'd give them the red carpet, but mind, we wouldn't stop for sore toes and blisters." He thumped his chest. "What do you say, sir? Am I your man?"

"I suppose you are, Mr. Crabb," said Arthur, with a moment's hesitation.

Later, as Arthur gathered supplies for the expedition, he met his son in the laboratory. "Will, it would be good to have you with us on this journey, but I realize you need to stay with your training."

"Are you sure it's wise to bring Lee Crabb on this journey?" Will asked.

"I don't trust him completely, but he is capable," said Arthur, tightly. "He owns a submersible down at Dolphin Bay that would serve our purposes."

"But isn't he just interested in riches?" Will persisted. "He seems like a treasure hunter."

"He probably is. But the bookkeeper sort is no help on a trip like this. I need a man with callouses on his hands."

"Then why bring Oriana?"

"I have no choice," said Arthur. "She comes with the key."

The chimes rang at the door. It was Bix, with a *Dimorphodon* messenger riding on her shoulder.

"Will, we've just spoken with Cirrus," said Bix, excitedly. "There has been a call for volunteer skybax riders on a dangerous mission."

"What is it?" Will asked.

"A convoy from Bonabba will soon be ready to cross the Rainy Basin. It's likely to be attacked."

"Tyrannosaurs!" said Will. "Can they ever be civilized? What can the skybax riders do?"

Will must leave on his own journey

*The Cargo Chute is
not often used for passengers*

"Fly cover, and in case of ambush, distract the tyrannosaurs," Bix replied. "Cirrus is ready, but only if you are, too."

"Absolutely!" Will exclaimed. He looked at Arthur.

"Very well," said his father. "This skybax riding will be a good stage in your training to become a real aeronaut. One day after you graduate from piloting beasts you will be captain of your own airship flying around the world."

"This is not a stage in my training, Father," Will said. "This is my life. And I owe my life to Cirrus." Someone called Will's name. "Father, I have to go."

"Go ahead then, with good speed," said Arthur. "Breathe deep."

"Seek peace," Will answered and left in haste to find his skybax.

Bix made a squeak. "Never underestimate a skybax, Arthur. One might save *your* life some day."

The next morning, two air-filled rubber boats bobbed at their moorings near the outlet of Pliosaur Canal. Arthur cut loose the rope on the first raft carrying supplies and sent it down the Cargo Chute. Then he joined the others in the second raft and plunged down into the rapids.

[31]

"We're in for heavy seas," said Crabb, as the first turn hurled them into a raging torrent. He uttered a yell of fear and defiance.

"Keep your head!" Arthur shouted to Crabb above the hiss and roar of the rapids. A heavy bump against the side sent Arthur sprawling into Oriana's lap. She hoisted him back up, much to his chagrin. When the current slowed for a moment, they wiped their faces and saw what they could of the tunnels in the basement of the city.

At last the canal opened to the sky. It hugged the cliff along Cloudbottom Gorge, and then dodged directly behind the curtain of Lower Thunder Falls.

Riding through the basement of Waterfall City

FOUR SOGGY TRAVELERS emerged from the Cargo Chute into the calmer waters of the Polongo River. The roar of the falls faded to a whisper. A slow, bubbling current carried them under the sunset and into the night. Crabb said they would soon arrive at a tavern where he docked his submersible. There they could dry off and refresh themselves.

The now oily water gave up a rotten smell of dead fish and dark muck. A pungent coal smoke stifled the air. Far off they heard low hoots, laughter, and breaking glass.

"There she be," said Crabb. "Black Fish Tavern. Flotsam and jetsam. Scalawags and scavengers. They're a scurvy lot, so mind you don't jabber about our little treasure hunt, or we'll have extra hands."

"This is not the kind of place for Miss Oriana," Arthur protested to Crabb.

Oriana intervened. "If it gets us on board our submersible, I shall be perfectly happy."

The building raised its scaly mass out of the water as if it had just surfaced, and might, at any minute, dive down again. The dock was lined with submersibles designed to scour the ocean floor in search of sunken treasure. Huddled in the flickering light were rough-hewn men, along with armored dinosaurs bristling with spines and scales.

Black Fish Tavern

[35]

Lee Crabb

"Lee Crabb, you black-hearted buccaneer!" shouted a voice from near the door.

"Ahoy, Mud Dog," responded Crabb, grinning. "Bless me, it's good to see the likes of you still helming a barnacle bucket."

"Are you making sport of me, you bottom feeder?" said Mud Dog. "I'm glad to clap an eye on you. That compass you swapped me wasn't worth the scrap. About time for you to settle—"

"Belay it. You're using up too much air," Crabb interrupted. "I want you to meet my lubberly mates here."

Mud Dog looked searchingly at Arthur. "And what be your business?" he said slowly.

Oriana spoke up. "We're biologists from Sauropolis. We are here to survey the population of trilobites. This gentleman is my assistant. And the *Protoceratops* is with us to brush up on her plesiosaur dialects."

"Is that so?" said Mud Dog. "Well, you're in for a fine ride, if you can hold your course and not let Lee Crabb steer you after gold. Here, we've got some grog for you. It's hard to come by on this island."

A dome-headed dinosaur waiter hobbled outside, carrying in its saddle pouches a set of drinking vessels made from giant ammonoid shells. Crabb and Mud Dog helped themselves to strong rum, while the rest sampled the ales made from *Pentoxylon* seeds.

The talk turned to the deadly currents of Dolphin Bay, the skeletons of old ship-wrecks there, the bone-plated giant fish who guards the best treasure, and the voyage of Cheng the Eel, an experienced treasure hunter who disappeared while searching for the Sunken Diamond Caves.

Oriana with a Pachycephalosaurus

A treasure-hunting submersible

"You're biologists, say you," Mud Dog continued. "Now how do you propose to find a submersible?"

"Well, that's it, Mud Dog," said Crabb. "I'd like to ask you for a small service, as I'm a bit light-ballasted in bullion. Could you let me borrow the *Remora* for just one day?"

Arthur was stunned. "Crabb, you said you *owned* a submersible."

"Well, I do—or did," stammered Crabb.

"You lost her to me fair and square," said Mud Dog. "The *Remora* is the best bucket in the fleet. You'll have to come up with a pretty pile of gold to buy her back, Crabb."

Sea stories by
lantern light

Mymoorapelta

Arthur stakes Crabb
in a gambling contest
called spinners.
Fortunately Crabb's luck
holds and he wins
back the Remora.

Bix has taught Oriana
how to say please
to a plesiosaur

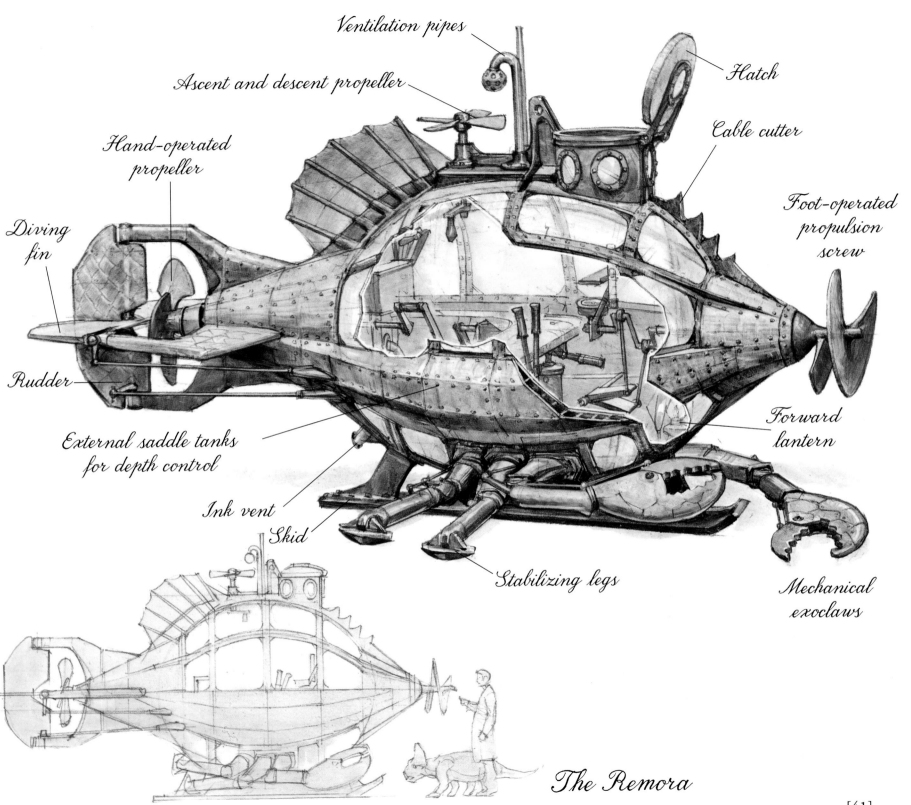

Ventilation pipes

Ascent and descent propeller

Hatch

Hand-operated propeller

Cable cutter

Diving fin

Foot-operated propulsion screw

Rudder

Forward lantern

External saddle tanks for depth control

Ink vent

Skid

Stabilizing legs

Mechanical exoclaws

The Remora

[41]

Arthur wondered whether Bix had told the other dinosaurs something about the quest they were to undertake. In any event, the creatures kept their own counsel. They sang a mournful melody of undulating pitches, which Arthur took to signify a kind of prayer for their journey.

[42]

The dragon flute's music calms fear or anger

Crabb found Arthur in the shadows of the moonlight. "We'd better slip our cables, captain, and shove off now. A news bird just blowed down from Waterfall City and spilled the whole tale about the key and the door. Now they're asking around if anyone has seen this Arthur Denison."

Learning that the sunken entrance to the caves was a long distance away—too far for most hand-powered submersibles—Oriana and Bix secretly arranged with several large sea reptiles at dockside to tow them for the first leg of the undersea voyage. Then, knowing that they would soon journey into the depths, they played a short farewell song to the moon and the stars.

Farewell to the moon

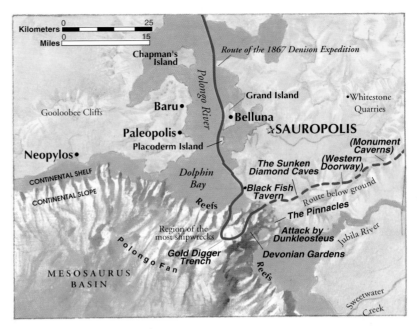

The seafloor near Dolphin Bay

"**T**HIS VESSEL DOESN'T LEAK, does it?" asked Bix nervously as they began the dive.

"Stow it, pinky," said Crabb. "The *Remora* has dug up more wrecks in more weather than Davy Jones himself. You won't find a barnacle bucket with better armor or bigger lungs. She'll hold us for at least five hours, even with you landlubbers gobbling up all the air."

With immense force the giant marine reptile flew through the water towing the *Remora*, her propellers disengaged to prevent them from freewheeling out of control. The submersible hugged the flat continental shelf and dove straight down into Gold Digger Trench.

A Kronosaurus tows the Remora

Devonian seafloor community

Ink lever

Depth gauge

Compass

Rudder control

Diving control

1. *Trilobite (Terataspis)*
2. *Nautiloid (Bactrites)*
3. *Crinoid (Ctenocrinus)*
4. *Brachiopod (Leptocoelia)*
5. *Colonial rugose coral*
6. *Solitary rugose coral*
7. *Trilobite (Calymene)*

The seafloor blossomed with a garden of living wonder: cone-shaped nautiloids and segmented trilobites drifting lazily through clusters of fragile sea lilies. Oriana, lying in the belly of the *Remora* with her hands operating the exoclaws, asked Crabb to please try to avoid the cloud of jellyfish ahead.

"I'm steering for it, sister. We need all the cover we can get. I don't want to be spotted by a hungry boneskull fish."

Dunkleosteus attacks the exoclaw

Suddenly a hard jolt from below sent the *Remora* heeling over, tossing the crew against the side. Crabb scrambled back to the controls.

"We've got our heads in a hornet's nest," said Crabb. "Denison, hit the ink lever." A black cloud gushed out. The sub lurched again.

"Something has got the claw!" shouted Oriana. She yanked her arms free from the mechanical claws just as the sound of tearing metal announced that the giant fish had sheared off one of the exo-claws at the elbow. They could see in dim outlines the two titans of the sea, *Kronosaurus* and

Dunkleosteus, circling and lunging at each other. The *Kronosaurus,* being an air breather, broke off the fight at last and swam upward out of sight.

Water had begun to leak in through the hole left by the missing claw. Oriana snatched a wad of oil-cloth and stuffed it in as a plug.

"We're on our own power now," said Arthur. "Our escort won't be coming back." He began working the rear propeller, while Crabb pedaled the front screw. When they paused to rest, they could hear far above them the muted rumble of the storm surf on rocky pinnacles.

They pressed on with only a half hour of breathable air remaining. The cabin grew stale and oppressive. Crabb brought the *Remora* coasting down over a graveyard of sunken galleons. With fascination, Arthur observed a group of creatures resembling giant swimming insects, which inhabited the bones of the wrecks.

"Crabb, what are you stopping for?" demanded Oriana.

"Never mind. Keep your eye on the sea bugs, and don't let them snag the props," said Crabb.

The submersible settled down by a wooden chest that was broken open, revealing a mound of gold. She grabbed his shoulder. "You can't stop here."

Crabb reached his arm into the remaining exoclaw. "Back off. I'll be just a minute."

Arthur rose from his seat, disturbed by Crabb's rudeness to Oriana. "Get back to the helm, Crabb. Right now," he said. "We'll all die down here if you don't come to your senses. Get moving, man."

Bix, ever the diplomat, intervened. "Look ahead! The mouth of the cave."

Eurypterids and nautiloids
live among the shipwrecks

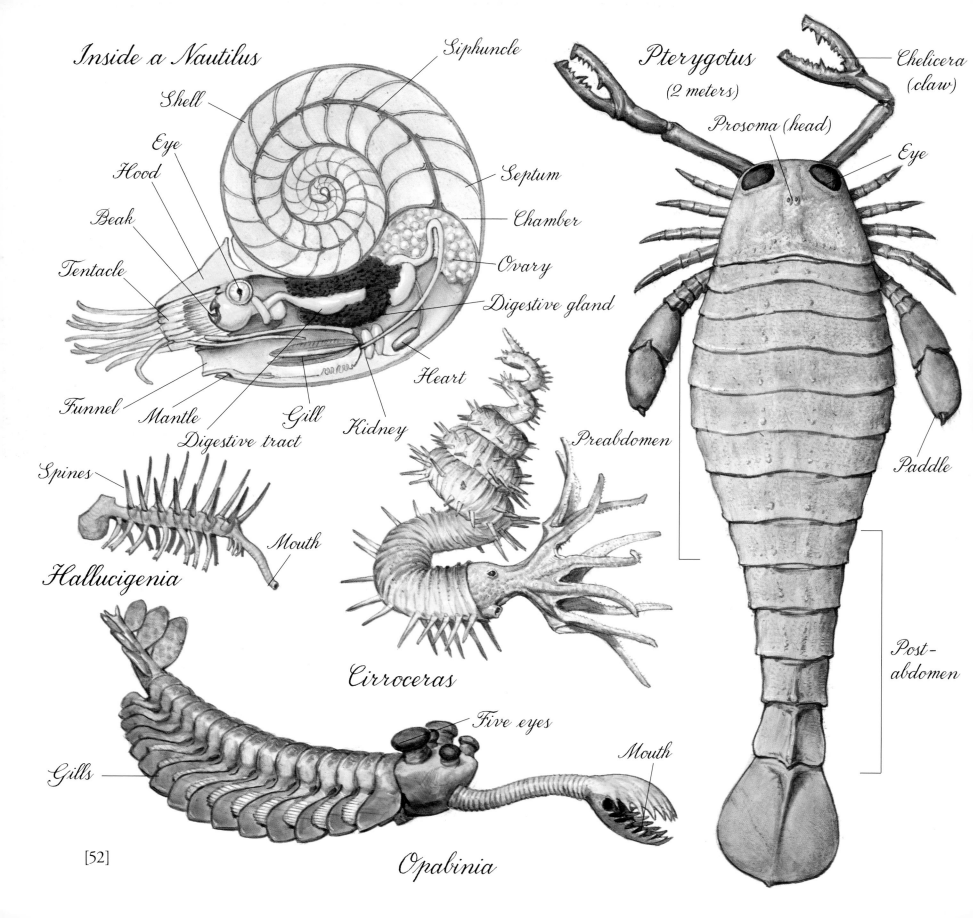

Inside a Nautilus

Siphuncle

Shell

Eye

Hood

Beak

Tentacle

Funnel

Mantle

Digestive tract

Gill

Kidney

Heart

Digestive gland

Ovary

Chamber

Septum

Pterygotus
(2 meters)

Chelicera
(claw)

Prosoma (head)

Eye

Paddle

Post-
abdomen

Preabdomen

Spines

Mouth

Hallucigenia

Cirroceras

Five eyes

Mouth

Gills

Opabinia

[52]

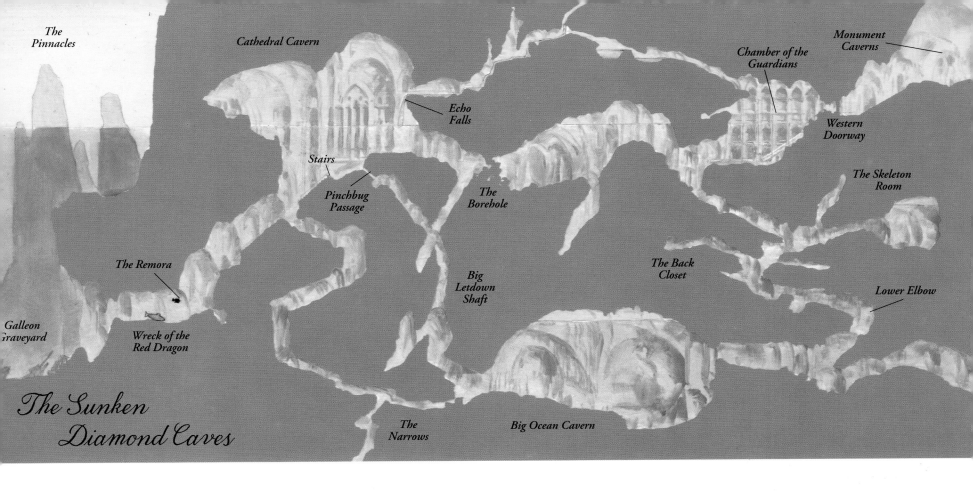

The Sunken Diamond Caves

The Pinnacles · Cathedral Cavern · Echo Falls · Chamber of the Guardians · Monument Caverns · Western Doorway · Stairs · Pinchbug Passage · The Borehole · The Skeleton Room · The Remora · Big Letdown Shaft · The Back Closet · Lower Elbow · Galleon Graveyard · Wreck of the Red Dragon · The Narrows · Big Ocean Cavern

Crabb pumped the saddle tanks full of what little reserve air was left, raising the *Remora* through the sunken tunnel. They grazed a wreck.

"It's another submersible!" said Oriana.

"So it be," said Crabb. "It's the *Red Dragon*. That was Cheng the Eel's last voyage. A good hand, but not good enough. So that's where he wound up."

After a long climb they surfaced and opened the hatch. The air was fresh enough to refill the sub's air tanks. Crabb felt confident igniting the forward lantern. But the light was hardly needed. The walls glowed with a dim phosphorescence that Arthur believed to be luminescent algae.

Massive columns and vaulted ceilings rose up into the shadows high above them. "Someone must have lived down here at one time," said Oriana, marveling at the surrounding cavern. Her words returned in a quiet echo.

"We've got company," said Crabb. A crowd of shellfish and arthropods gathered around the sub. Crabb made ready to attack them with the remaining claw, but Bix intervened, suggesting that they wait and try to read their intention. The creatures pressed their expressionless eyes to the glass and watched the crew with neither malice nor compassion. Some hovered near the glass, dull and imperturbable, while others darted off into the darkness of the caves.

"Let's follow them," said Bix. "They can help us. They may know the way through the maze."

After a long journey through underwater passages, the *Remora* surfaced in a grand chamber. They disembarked. Crabb grinned at Arthur. "So this is the door that stumped you, eh, Professor?"

"It's as far as Bix and I ever got."

Oriana stepped beside Arthur and said, "Will you please give me the other half of the key?"

"Young woman, I really don't think—"

"Oh, don't worry. You'll get it back."

When Crabb started kicking at the door, Arthur relented and handed Oriana the key. She fitted the two parts together and placed the completed key in his hands, with hers briefly cupped around his.

Moments later the lock yielded with a squeak and a clank, and the doors swung toward them, pushed open by a warm breeze. No one had expected the view that opened before them: a shining landscape of glimmering pools and vast towers shaped by Nature's hand. Bix cooed. Arthur wished his son could be with him for this triumphant moment. Oriana felt a deep recognition, as if seeing a childhood home again.

"I'll be dunked in rum!" Crabb shouted gleefully.

Chamber of the Guardians

As Arthur's expedition enters the World Beneath,
Will patrols the Rainy Basin

AT THAT VERY MOMENT, Will was flying on his skybax, Cirrus, scouting high above the Rainy Basin in search of tyrannosaurs. The clouds were magnificent. His skybax rolled to one side and dove directly into a billowing cumulus. While immersed in the whiteness, Will thought of his father far below. His skybax let out a cry and then exploded into the sunshine above Bonabba.

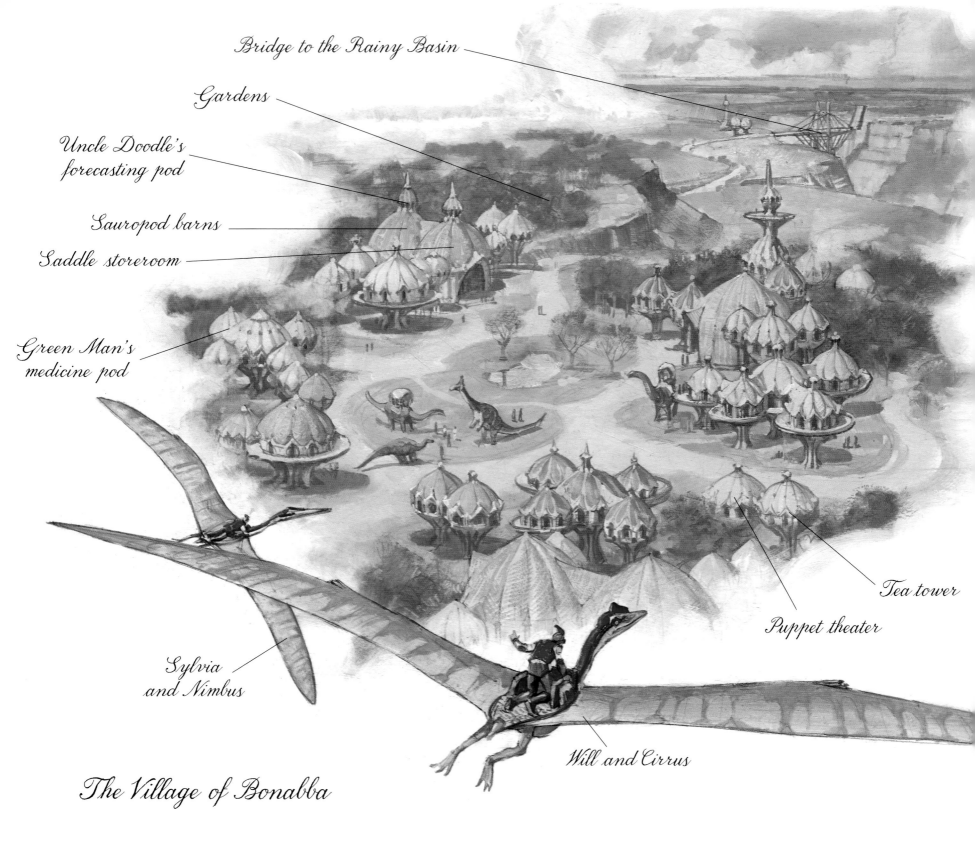

Bridge to the Rainy Basin

Gardens

Uncle Doodle's
forecasting pod

Sauropod barns

Saddle storeroom

Green Man's
medicine pod

Tea tower

Puppet theater

Sylvia
and Nimbus

Will and Cirrus

The Village of Bonabba

He unsaddled his skybax and looked out over his new temporary home. The sleepy village had come to life in recent weeks in preparation for the spring convoy of armored sauropods, which would soon cross over the bridge to the Rainy Basin and carry out its various missions of trade and diplomacy.

Until then, Will and Sylvia, along with the rest of the skybax riders, had kept to a routine of hard exercises and disciplined training. But there was plenty of free time for high spirits and good-natured practical jokes, usually directed toward members of the sauropod clan, who rode high above the ground on majestic brachiosaurs.

For Will and Sylvia, it was a time of anticipation of the dangers to come, and celebration of the joys at hand.

Will and Sylvia

Will swooped low over the pod-shaped buildings of Bonabba. He was followed by Sylvia Romano, his friend since he was first shipwrecked on Dinotopia, and now an apprentice skybax rider just like himself. The skybaxes approached the roosting tower and fanned their wings to act as air brakes.

"No sightings in Moss Valley," Will reported to the survey captain on the platform. "But Sylvia saw part of the tyrannosaur pack over in Bogpeat Marsh."

Ulf Jensen of the sauropod clan

[61]

Bonabba Pod House

Chimney

Moss and lichen

Boarding platform

Message sandbox

Stove

Door

Ladder

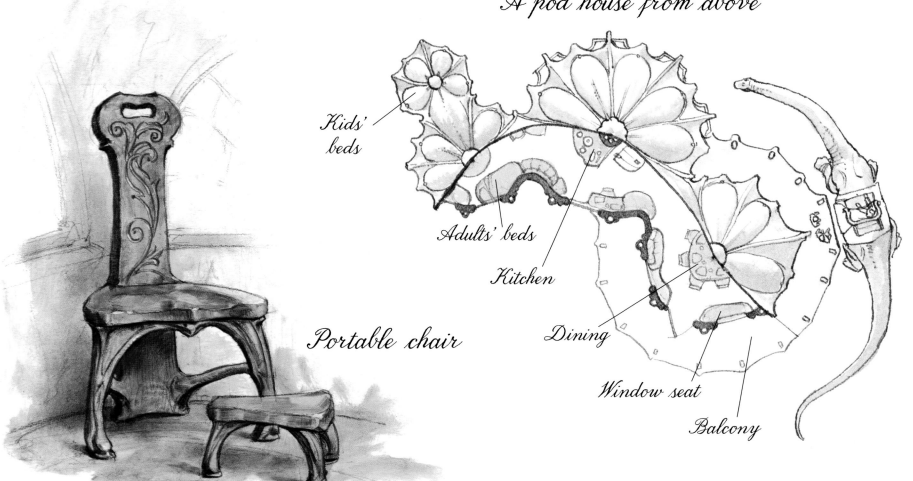

A pod house from above

Kids' beds

Adults' beds

Kitchen

Dining

Window seat

Balcony

Portable chair

Sign near a doorway

Teapot

Uncle Doodle, forecaster of Bonabba, with his
Rhamphorhynchoid companion, Pipsqueak

They predict fortunes and
anticipate weather, but guess
wrong most of the time

The Triceratops likes
to wear a human
just as a human
likes to wear
a hat

A Struthiomimus tour guide

During springtime festivals the Green Man walks through the village as children try to pluck the flowers from his belt

A tale called "Little Simon and the Tyrannosaur"

On a typical evening, Will enjoyed sitting by the firelight to watch a puppet show. Children gathered around him affectionately. He was a favorite among the younger ones because he always remembered to bring them colorful beads or little animal figurines that he had found while exploring some faraway ruins.

"Quiet, everyone," called a voice as the puppet show began. The hero, a boy named Little Simon, heads into the jungle looking for treasure. Along the way he offers his piece of bread to an old *Archaeopteryx*. The bird thanks him, and gives him a bag of sticky beans. Next, a tyrannosaur threatens to eat Little Simon. Knowing the tyrannosaur's greedy nature, Simon tells him he has a bag of the world's sweetest candy. The tyrannosaur may have some, if he eats his main course of Little Simon first. Instead, the dinosaur demands the dessert. Its jaws are glued shut by the sticky candy, and Little Simon runs off with a treasure trove of diamonds.

Molokito, maker of sunshine

Igg Jaggly, the tooth trader, swaps seashells for teeth

The skybax represents the silent observer

The tyrannosaur is seen as greedy and angry

Masked dancers appear in every festival

[67]

A boy and a Styracosaurus
alongside the
Laguthar River

A Camarasaurus leads
a picnic excursion into
Slumberbund Valley

*Dinosaurs and humans alike
relish an occasional
"do-nothing" afternoon*

*Will Denison helps inspire
the popular sport among skybax
riders called the "flying start"*

Pear blossoms

IN SPRING, AS IN YOUTH, all things point away from home: the root from the seed, the child from the hearth, and the hatchling from the shell, each knowing nothing of October. In Bonabba's hatchery, one young *Triceratops* came away from his eggshell blinking feebly amid the preparations for the convoy. His given name was Strongbrow of the Line of Grayback, but Will nicknamed him Stubbs and said he looked very much like his grandfather Brokehorn, who was already on his way to meet his first grandhatchling.

But Stubbs had taken ill. He refused most food. Music and fresh garden air did little to stir him.

Rosemary, Zeke, and Thistlebud
present the new hatchling, Stubbs

Stubbs brightens at the
greeting "Breathe deep, seek peace,"
but it has no lasting effect

Lawana

Meg

Zeke

The children take turns
looking after him

Seeking a
cure for Stubbs,
Sylvia joins
a twilight
procession
through the
Garden
of Hope

Inside the sauropod barns

The night before the convoy was to depart, the giant dinosaurs gathered inside the sauropod barns to be fitted for their armor. Meanwhile, nearby, the herbalist doctor known as the Green Man was rummaging through his vast collection of plant medicines, looking for something to help Stubbs, who had now grown lethargic and unresponsive. Nothing helped, not even the reliable remedies of *Echinacea*, *Hydrastis*, and *Arctium*.

Only one medicine seemed to work, and it was in short supply: the extract of the silicon-rich *Calamite*, or horsetail tree. According to the Green Man, the rare species grew only in the Rainy Basin, and might well be found along the convoy route. If, despite the tyrannosaurs, a good quantity of the tree could be harvested and brought back by the armored sauropods, then Stubbs might be healed and Brokehorn's lineage ensured.

Will and Sylvia received their assignment: fly close enough to the convoy to distract the tyrannosaurs in case of attack, but keep a careful watch for the horsetail tree.

The last of the medicine made from the rare horsetail tree

At the first light of morning, Will climbed the spiral ladder to the skybax roost. Cirrus was sleeping with his huge head tucked into his wings. As the great creature awoke and stretched, Will looked eastward out the round window. A long silk banner outside had begun to stir in the warm wind that was drifting over from the Rainy Basin. The wind brought with it exotic aromas of the jungle, which called forth something deep in Will: a sense of yearning, a hunger for adventure.

Cirrus rested his gigantic beak on Will's shoulder, his way of asking for his neck to be scratched. "Come on, sleepyhead," said Will. "We've got a big job ahead of us."

Cirrus and Will

Will reached for the skybax saddle, which was as light as a basket but as strong as a work boot. As he buckled it on, he said, "I hope you know what a horsetail tree looks like, because I don't. If you see one, let me know. Let's be the first to find one."

Cirrus gave a low trill of agreement.

"Denison," called a voice from below the flight platform, "we're moving out." It was Ulf Jensen, riding high on the neck of a fully armored brachiosaur. "Ready to be tyrannosaur bait?"

"Right," Will replied. "At least I'll taste better than you with all that tin you're wearing."

A young brachiosaur in full armor

[79]

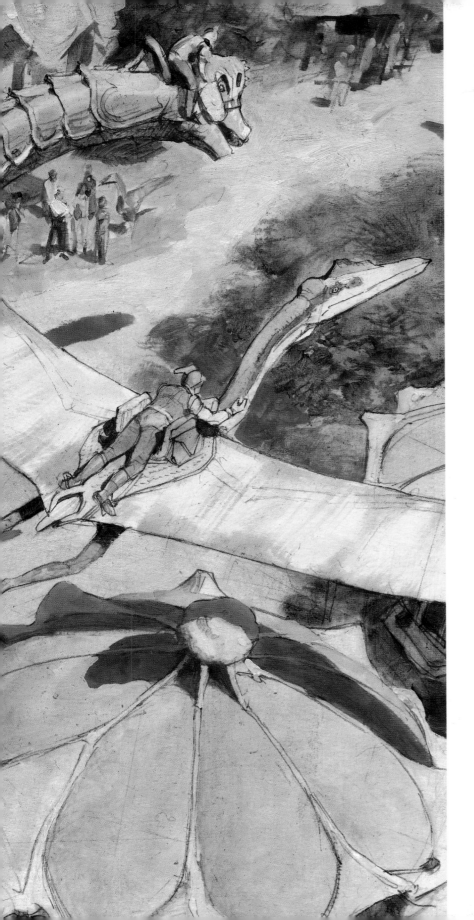

Into the realm of the tyrannosaurs

By noon the convoy gathered its important passengers and departed Bonabba, soon crossing the drawbridge into the Rainy Basin. The plan was to spend the night at a stockade near Bogpeat Marsh, the first safe point on the Cross Basin Trail. Generally the tyrannosaurs could be kept at bay with offerings of smoked fish. But appeasement might not suffice for gaining permission to harvest medicinal plants.

"If only Bix were here to be our negotiator," said one of the convoy members.

Sylvia and Nimbus circled close to the armored brachiosaur, alert for ambush. Will and Cirrus scouted ahead along the trail, but saw no tyrannosaurs. "We've gone far enough," said Will. "Shouldn't we turn around?" The skybax angled to the side. "Where are you taking me?" Will asked. "Do you see a horsetail tree?"

A stairway leads up to a palace

*Each doorway is crowned
with strange carvings*

Cirrus glided toward a place in the jungle where the tree canopy formed a mound.

"What are you doing? This is no time for stunts!" Will yelled as his skybax dodged through the tree-tops and landed on a stone ledge. All around them, hidden among tangled growth, dark and forlorn towers revealed their outlines. "What kind of place is this?" Will said aloud. His forehead beaded up with sweat in the still air.

"Can you follow me up these stairs?" he asked. Cirrus scrambled awkwardly behind him like a folded kite. Never mind the horsetail trees for now, Will thought. The lure of the massive ruins overpowered him. He squinted at carvings above a doorway showing a race of snake-tailed humans emerging from the mouths of tyrannosaurs and allosaurs. On the ground beside him was a mask blending human and saurian features.

Suddenly the ground began to rumble. Cirrus screamed and spread his wings.

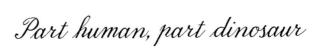

Part human, part dinosaur

"Don't leave without me!" Will shouted, as Cirrus struggled to take off. Will's heart was racing. He sucked air into his lungs and leapt outward, almost overshooting. At the moment his chest thumped into the saddle, the clash of teeth rattled behind him.

Cirrus pumped the air until they cleared the trees and skimmed above the canopy. Now Will heard roaring ahead. Obviously the convoy was in trouble. He muttered to himself, "I shouldn't have been gone so long." And to Cirrus, "Fly low and let them almost get us. Distract them. Don't let them circle the convoy, or all will be lost."

As they streaked for the convoy, Will prayed Sylvia was safe and that he would get a chance to see his father again.

*Last-minute dive
to the saddle*

Lost in a cavern wilderness

"WHY DON'T YOU ADMIT you've busted a rudder, Professor?" said Lee Crabb. "You've got us all lost in this devil dungeon. We'll all end up dead instead of rich, like Cheng the Eel, with no mother to mourn us."

"Enough, Crabb," said Oriana. "If your sore feet

hadn't kept us from jumping across that chasm, I'm sure we would have been able to stay along the main route. Now we have no choice but to see this way through."

Arthur stopped to admire a chandelier of gypsum stalactites. "Any one of these formations would make a cave famous in the rest of the world. I know geologists who would endure the journey just to see the cave pearls and aragonite trees we discovered this morning."

"Cave pearls ain't worth a sockful of sand in the swap market," grumbled Crabb.

Lee Crabb

Arthur Denison

Oriana

Bix

"This is no dungeon, Mr. Crabb," said Bix, "unless you make it one. We dinosaurs respect the caverns because they saved our lives. Millions of years ago—long before our human friends arrived—there was a terrible storm, with black clouds that covered the sun. During the years that the clouds remained, these caves were our only refuge."

"Spare me the fairy tale, flat top. This is no Garden of Eden. All I've seen so far are dead ships and skeletons. But where there's bones, there's treasure."

"I think you're both right in a way," said Oriana as they continued along the trail, passing a forest of stone columns. "This is a place of death, but also of life. After passing through this darkness, one can emerge again as if being newly reborn."

She came alongside Arthur. "You, for example, Mr. Denison. You undertook this journey to begin your life again, didn't you?"

"Me? Nonsense," Arthur said, rubbing his moustache and looking doubtfully at Oriana. "It has nothing to do with me, personally. I am only interested in the objective facts. The only thing that will be born here will be scientific understanding. And the only thing that will die will be myth and superstition."

"Myth will never die," said Oriana. "It is the deepest kind of understanding."

They carried on in silence for a time, forced by the labor of the trail to keep their attention on their hands and feet. They inched their way up great cliffs of flowstone, balanced along the slippery narrow edge of limestone bowls, dropped down by rope into yawning gulfs, and skipped across thundering waters that cascaded into the bowels of the earth.

High Hopes Falls and the Stone Forest

The maze of caverns led them on into a gallery of natural stone sculptures. Arthur stopped before one of them.

"It's a typical calcite formation." He touched the glistening surface. "Do you see how the water drips here? It has been dripping here for countless centuries. Each droplet contains a tiny bit of dissolved limestone. The effect of millions of droplets over time has been to create this random accretion, following the laws of chance."

"You say it's chance," said Crabb, narrowing his eyes at the formation. "I say it's plain bad luck, flat and simple. Do you see what it is? It's the skull of a dead man, bugging his eyes at us."

"How can you say that?" said Oriana. "There's no skull. It's clearly a woman holding her baby, with two other children beside her."

"We all find what we expect to find," said Bix, "as long as we see with our hearts as much as with our eyes."

What Lee Crabb sees　　　　　　　　　　　　　*What Oriana sees*

[93]

"Too big to be diamonds"

Types of Sunstones

Crystal system: hexagonal
Hardness: 11, Specific gravity: 3.6
Piezoelectric and reverse refractive properties

They continued on, passing into a cavern as large as a valley, with a sparkling ceiling high above. Before them stood a mountainous crystalline formation composed of countless shining stones.

"Too big to be diamonds," said Crabb.

"These must be sunstones in their natural state," replied Arthur. "The ancient scrolls called this place the bed of the sun. The mines of Ogthar. Enough sunstones to power a hundred cities!"

Oriana wandered to a place where she could be alone. She closed her eyes. As smoke rises from glowing embers, images arose from the sunstones. A gentle voice addressed her. She saw a figure both strange and familiar, a figure whom she knew to be her own mother. The woman in the vision flickered. Her face changed from one individual to another, yet always resembled Oriana. The garments became more and more ancient. At last the entire vision dissolved into a swirl of shimmering vapors. Oriana realized that she had witnessed her own chain of maternal ancestors, whose faces till then were unknown to her.

Vision in the sunstone mines

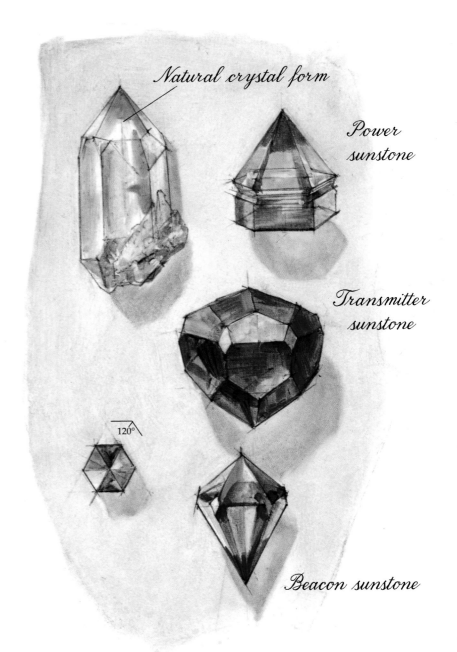

Natural crystal form

Power sunstone

Transmitter sunstone

120°

Beacon sunstone

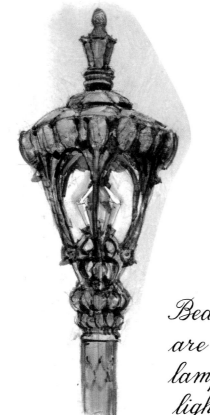

Giant ferns uncoil in the presence of the sunstone

Beacon sunstones are used in lamps and lighthouses

Among the debris of the mines were heavy wagons, some still loaded with a harvest of raw sunstones. Crabb found a stack of wooden crates and pried off a lid. Inside was a black dust which Crabb at first believed to be gunpowder. Bix maintained that it was a supply of fern spores that had long lain dormant.

"How do I know it's not just sand?" asked Crabb, taking a handful and scattering it over the soft powder of the cave floor.

Suddenly there arose little puffs of dust all around them. Spiral tendrils of giant ferns sprouted from the ground and uncoiled slowly into a lush garden.

[96]

(Twice actual size)

They ventured into a labyrinth of tunnels. At every turn were niches where offerings had been placed. Arthur picked up a statuette and found the following name inscribed underneath it:

↑↓⇇⇇↓⇉

"So this is Ogthar," he said. "The legendary king of Poseidos. Half human and half—" he turned inquiringly to Bix.

"Ceratopsian," she said proudly. "The name refers to a big family. We're known for the frills that adorn our heads. When you combine human and ceratopsian qualities, you get a race of creatures called 'anthroceratops,' renowned for great powers of wisdom."

"Which half contributes the wisdom?" Arthur asked. "Never mind; don't tell me," he said, laughing.

Passing through a narrow tunnel, they came upon a remarkable discovery unlike anything they had ever seen in Dinotopia: a gigantic mechanical leg, discarded and lifeless. Arthur was electrified with excitement. He ran his hands over it as a doctor would, muttering "Magnificent!" again and again. By chance he brought a sunstone near it. The leg twitched at the knee and the ankle. For just a moment they heard faint clicking sounds from within the leg.

Ogthar, with a leaf-shaped frill, seated on a lotus throne, holding a gilded sunstone with a flame motif

Discovery of the mechanical leg

Deeper and deeper they traveled into the very heart of the earth. One chamber led into another, through vaulted passages shaped by an unknown art, and illuminated by a mysterious radiance.

"I believe this was a laboratory of some kind," said Arthur, "perhaps where sunstones were shaped."

Bix said, "Barges, canals, roads. Do you see? This was also a place of transport and storage."

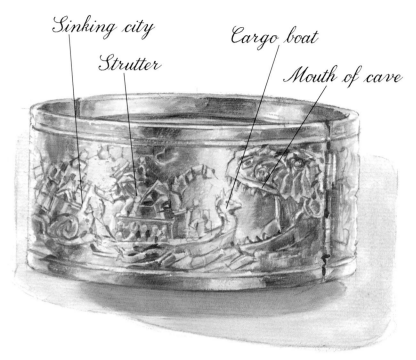

Sinking city
Strutter
Cargo boat
Mouth of cave

Decorations on a bracelet

Not much remains of the treasure

CRABB'S MIND WAS FIXED on one thing, the legendary treasure given away by King Ogthar. He bounded ahead and quickly found a room where it seemed the treasure had once been locked away. But there was no need of a key this time. Something had torn open the doors with immense force and taken away the treasure, leaving only a few jewels and ornaments of little value. Crabb stuffed them in his pack and strode away, grumbling loudly about their bad luck and wasted effort.

Arthur explored ahead. He peered into a sunken courtyard. "Look here!" he called. "A whole fleet of machines. They look as though they once could strut around under their own power. Strutters! Marvelous! Why were they abandoned?"

*The floor is crowded with strutters,
strange vehicles abandoned
for centuries*

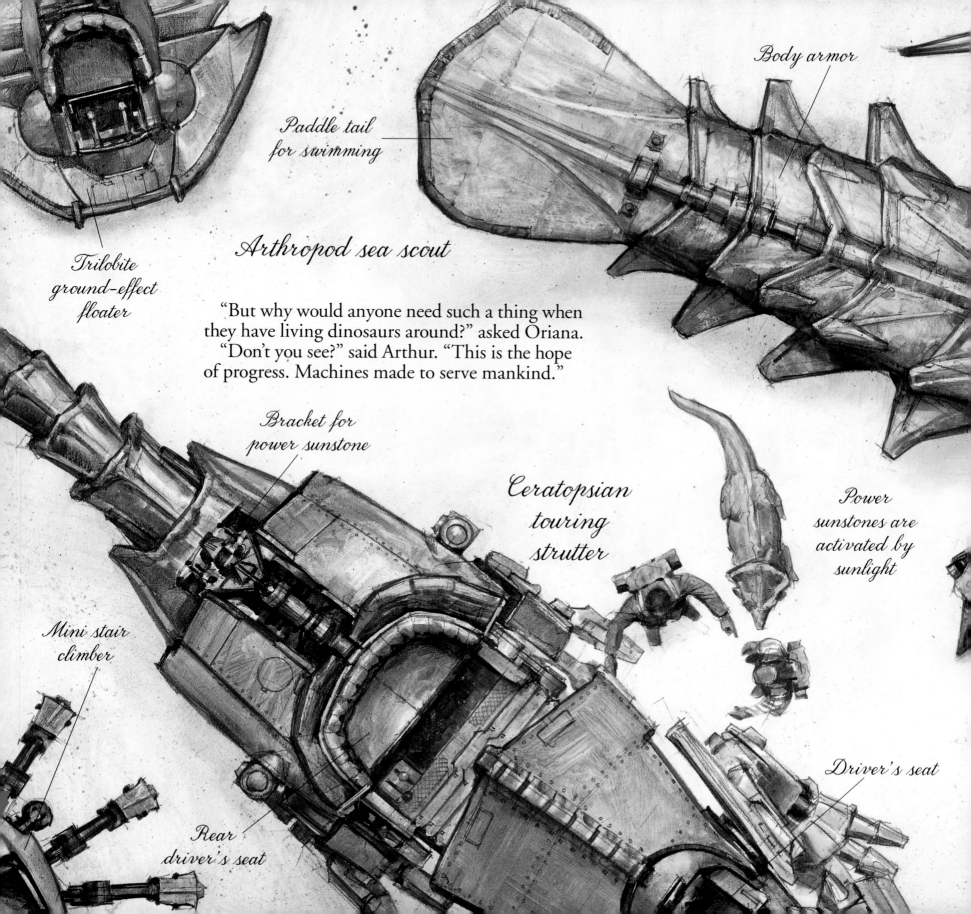

Trilobite
ground-effect
floater

Paddle tail
for swimming

Body armor

Arthropod sea scout

"But why would anyone need such a thing when they have living dinosaurs around?" asked Oriana. "Don't you see?" said Arthur. "This is the hope of progress. Machines made to serve mankind."

Bracket for
power sunstone

Ceratopsian
touring
strutter

Power
sunstones are
activated by
sunlight

Mini stair
climber

Driver's seat

Rear
driver's seat

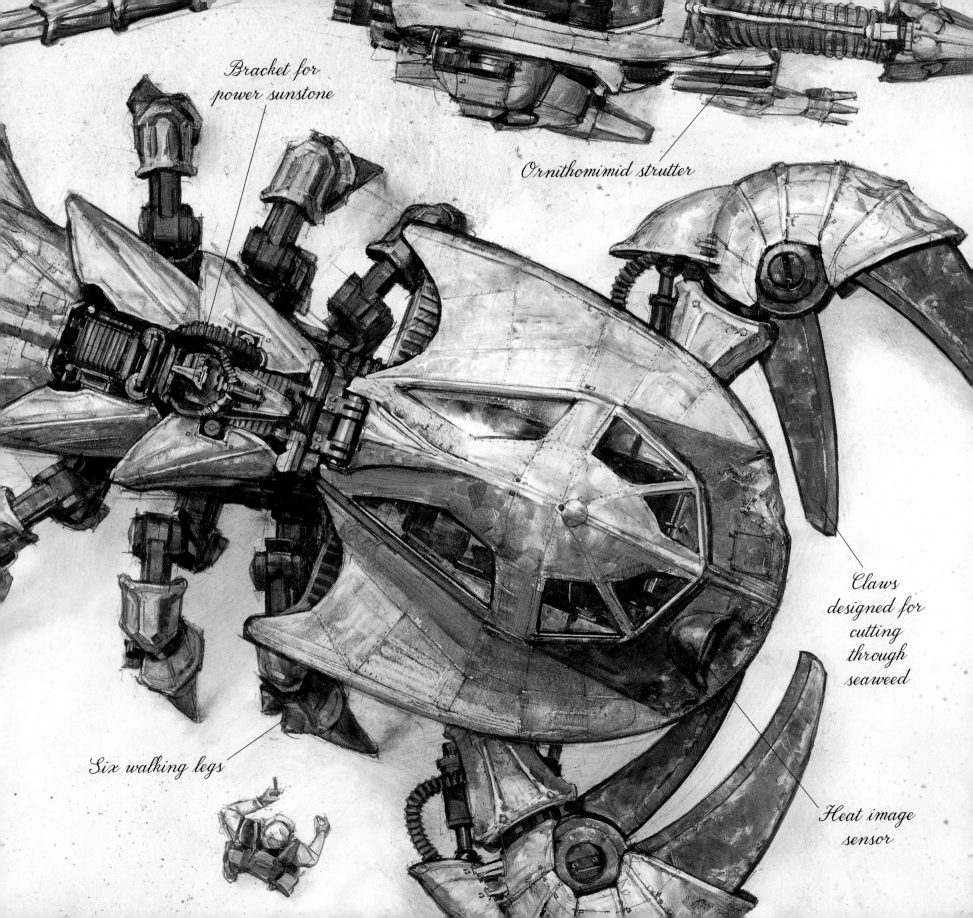

Bracket for
power sunstone

Ornithomimid strutter

Claws
designed for
cutting
through
seaweed

Six walking legs

Heat image
sensor

Loading a power sunstone

"These machines seem to be waiting in readiness," said Arthur. "Apparently the sunstone has some power over them." He lifted one of the stones, which lay in racks nearby, and slowly moved it over the surface of what looked like a touring strutter. The vehicle shivered. After many minutes of experimentation, he found a bracket where the sunstone could be loaded, and he clamped it in place. There was a sound like breathing.

"The sunstones are weak," said Oriana. "They need to be fed with light to have any stength. Look, you can see a ray touching the top of that tower. If one of us can rotate that transmitter stone, we can bring the beam of light down here."

"I'll go aloft," said Crabb, winking at Oriana. "Climbing that tower is no trouble at all for a fine physical specimen like myself," he said. He spat into his hands, rubbed them together, and began to climb the tower while Arthur loaded more sunstones.

Crabb reached the top and swiveled the mechanism. A ray of light pierced the gloom, touching the backs of the machines. A strutter in the form of an arthropod shook itself like a creature roused from an uneasy sleep.

"I wonder if it communicates," said Bix, who began to chirp eagerly.

The machine lifted a flap on its side and let out a loud, rattling blast of stale air. Bix backed off. "What a crude, ill-mannered beast," she said.

*Crabb directs the light beam
to activate the strutters*

Crabb came down from the tower. "When I was up there in the crow's nest," he said, "I could see a pathway whittled out of the rock. It seems to head upward, right alongside the shaft of light. It ain't no boulevard, but I bet we can march a couple of these strutters out of here."

"Shouldn't we all ride together?" asked Bix.

"One strutter may not take us all the way out," reasoned Crabb. "Let's take two, and if one gets stuck we can all ride in the other."

He settled into his cockpit. As if by second nature, Lee Crabb began working the giant claws. "Wouldn't Grampa Crabb love to see me now?" he said to himself through clenched teeth.

Arthur climbed into the cockpit pod of the touring strutter. He turned to Oriana and said playfully, "Where may I drive your coach, madam?"

"To the surface of the world, if you please, sir," she replied. "But you know, Arthur, you're not the only one driving. I have controls back here, too." She tested the two brass handles, rocking them back and forth. The machine straightened its back legs with a jerk, bouncing like a playful dog.

Bix looked queasy. "Oh, what I would give for a nice soft nest of ferns."

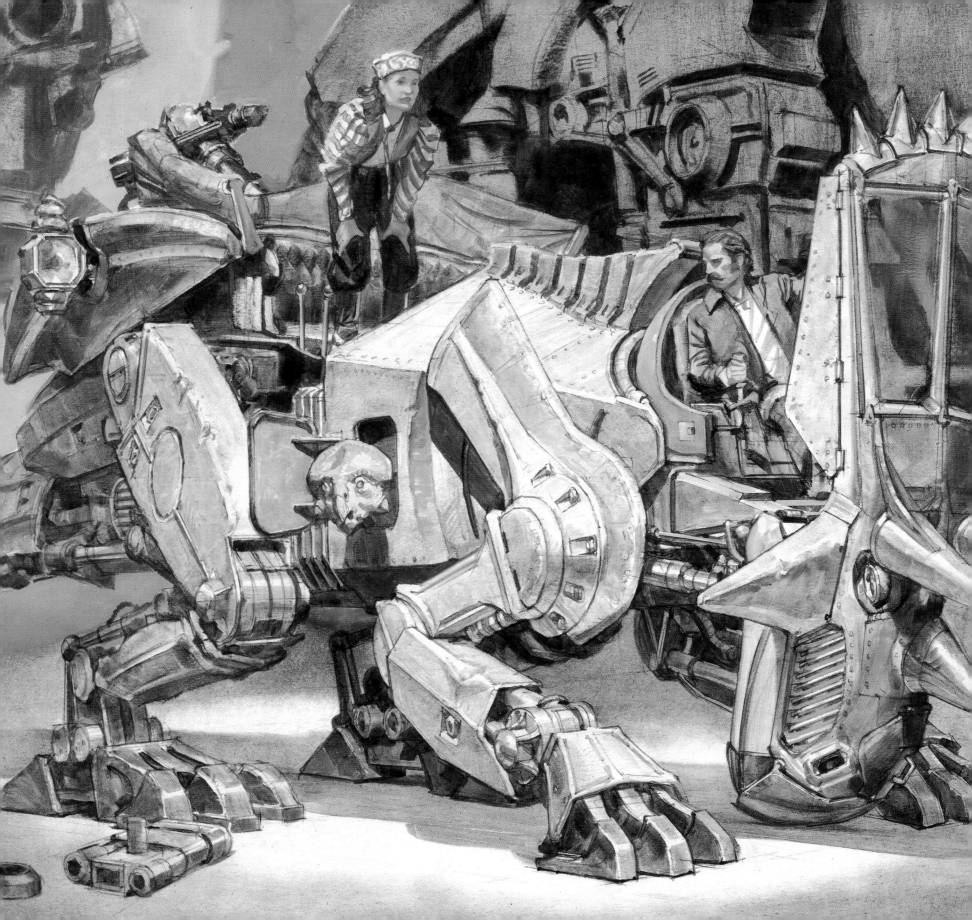

Having legs instead of wheels allowed the strutters to climb stairs and jump across narrow gaps with little difficulty. But there were many hazards. On a slippery flowstone stairway, large boulders rolled loose and almost crushed them. The strutter's agility impressed Arthur. He turned to Bix and said thoughtlessly, "Aren't these better than dinosaurs?"

"I'm sure they're more considerate than humans," she muttered.

"I get the feeling we're close to the exit," said Oriana. "I smell a jungle."

"Yes, jungle," returned Bix, sniffing suspiciously. "If we come out in the Rainy Basin, we mustn't expect a welcoming committee."

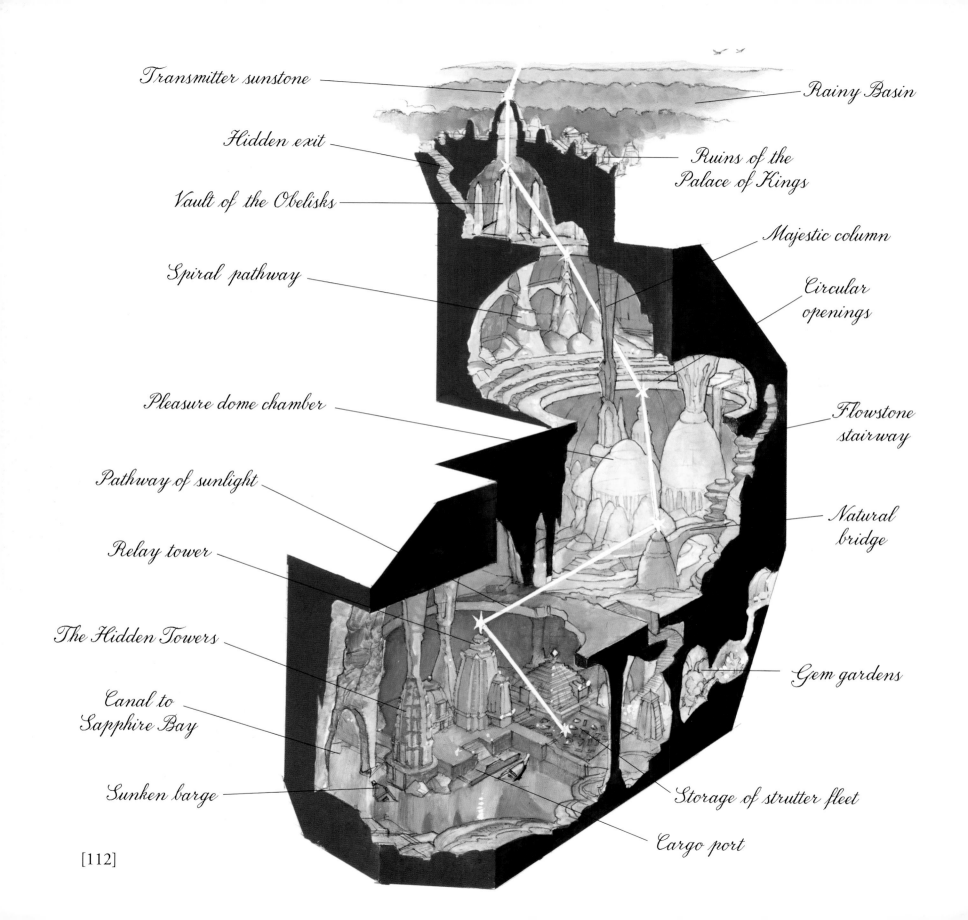

Transmitter sunstone

Hidden exit

Vault of the Obelisks

Spiral pathway

Pleasure dome chamber

Pathway of sunlight

Relay tower

The Hidden Towers

Canal to Sapphire Bay

Sunken barge

Rainy Basin

Ruins of the Palace of Kings

Majestic column

Circular openings

Flowstone stairway

Natural bridge

Gem gardens

Storage of strutter fleet

Cargo port

[112]

The lost gardens

THE EXIT FROM THE CAVES was a hidden stairway that led into the midst of an overgrown ruin. They stopped for a moment to refresh themselves alongside a pool. Suddenly they heard a rustling noise in the nearby bushes.

"Who goes there?" Arthur demanded.

It showed itself to be a styracosaur. "Do you know where you are, travelers?" it said with some alarm.

"We know we are not in Sauropolis," said Bix. "Perhaps you can tell us. May we ask your name?"

"I am Degdah, advance guard of the convoy from Bonabba." Arthur and Bix exchanged glances as Degdah continued. "We are returning with full freight and passengers, along with medicine for a sick hatchling. Friends, you had better stay with us; the tyrannosaurs are angry here."

They joined the convoy for a time, wading into a shallow river to mask their scent. But they had stumbled into an ambush of tyrannosaurs and allosaurs, who soon surrounded Arthur's strutter. There was little the rest of the convoy could do to help. Crabb's strutter swam away, abandoning them. The styracosaurs did their best to sow confusion. Nevertheless, with a cold fire in his eye, a tyrannosaur placed a heavy foot on the machine while Arthur fumbled with the control handles.

The tyrannosaur rips loose the head

A narrow escape

In a single, swift movement the dinosaur tore loose the head from the strutter and swung it away. Bix scrambled into the stowage cabin, popping out her head from the relative safety of the hatch.

The headless strutter reared up on its back legs, flailing its front legs like a horse. For a moment the tyrannosaur blinked and stepped back.

"Arthur, get it going!" Oriana shouted.

"I'm trying!" he cried as he kicked it into gear and shoved the handles forward. The strutter lunged ahead with tremendous energy. It dodged and ducked through a maze of vegetation, galloping just ahead of the tyrannosaurs as it approached the rising gate of the drawbridge.

A bold leap to the drawbridge returned them to safety. Their hearts pounded as they watched the tyrannosaurs turn back. Far away the jungle echoed with unearthly howls.

"A close call back there," said Bix.

"A little too close," said Arthur. "Why did the meat-eaters attack us? Were they hungry?"

"No, I don't think so. They easily could have eaten us."

"Maybe they didn't like the strutters."

"Yes, or perhaps they didn't like us being in that part of the jungle," Bix said.

"I wonder if they were guarding something."

"They might have been defending their young. Brokehorn tells me they are very protective parents."

"How does Brokehorn know about them?" asked Arthur.

"He lived for many years as a hermit in the Rainy Basin. But not long ago, a powerful new leader took over among the tyrannosaurs, and Brokehorn was forced to leave."

Before long they heard the sounds of drums and singing, and they smelled the rich aroma of baking bread.

Safe in Bonabba

*Brokehorn arrives to find
Stubbs returning to health*

Bonabba was in a flurry of excitement as the jungle-weary convoy arrived. Villagers gathered to help remove the armor from the sauropods. The Green Man unloaded the medicinal plants and prepared the cure for Stubbs, whose verve and color soon returned under the watchful care of all the children.

At the great celebration feast, Brokehorn thanked everyone for their heroism. Reunited again, Arthur and Will joyfully watched dancers wearing tyrannosaur costumes reenacting the thrilling stories of the chase.

But Crabb seemed restless. He forced a smile and bowed when honored at the feast, but otherwise kept to himself.

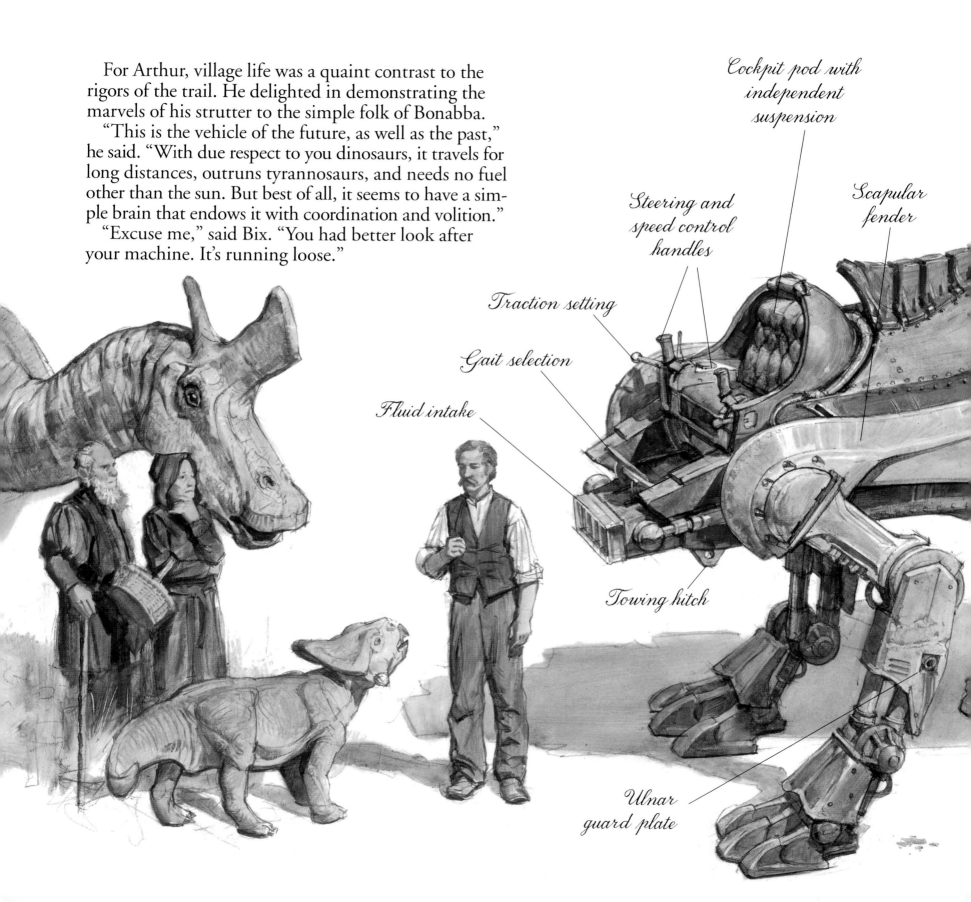

For Arthur, village life was a quaint contrast to the rigors of the trail. He delighted in demonstrating the marvels of his strutter to the simple folk of Bonabba.

"This is the vehicle of the future, as well as the past," he said. "With due respect to you dinosaurs, it travels for long distances, outruns tyrannosaurs, and needs no fuel other than the sun. But best of all, it seems to have a simple brain that endows it with coordination and volition."

"Excuse me," said Bix. "You had better look after your machine. It's running loose."

Cockpit pod with independent suspension

Scapular fender

Steering and speed control handles

Traction setting

Gait selection

Fluid intake

Towing hitch

Ulnar guard plate

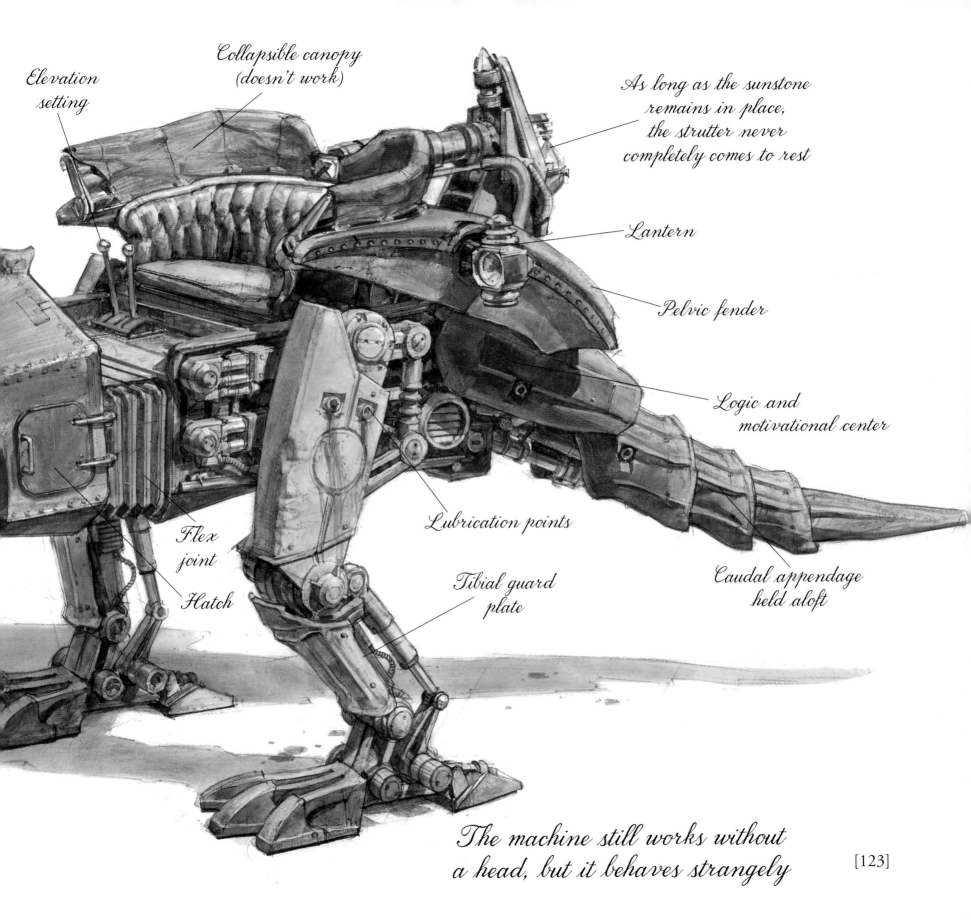

Elevation setting

Collapsible canopy (doesn't work)

As long as the sunstone remains in place, the strutter never completely comes to rest

Lantern

Pelvic fender

Logic and motivational center

Lubrication points

Caudal appendage held aloft

Flex joint

Hatch

Tibial guard plate

The machine still works without a head, but it behaves strangely

[123]

Arthur's strutter acts as if it has a mind of its own

Gulping water for cooling

Tracking mud and knocking about

Plowing heedlessly through picnics and flower gardens

Come back!

Only by removing the sunstone can the strutter be fully immobilized

Tail slowly wags to a stop

[125]

"The golden age is here right now"

Oriana found Arthur feeling embarrassed. "Don't worry," she said. "No one blames you for the machine's mischief. All is cleaned up and forgiven." She smiled. "Actually, I think you gave everyone some real amusement."

"But don't you see the miracle of this ancient science, Oriana? Those engineers created machines on the verge of life, with real personalities. If we can tame them, harness them for the good of this island, we can bring back a golden age to Dinotopia, an age without vulgarity and drudgery."

"The golden age is here right now," said Oriana. "You just don't see it. No engineer ever invented anything as miraculous as a flower or an egg or a living dinosaur. It's never drudgery to live among them."

"But you can't live like animals. What about the roof over your head and the shoes on your feet? Aren't those inventions?"

"Yes, indeed, true conveniences. But for anything gained, something else is given away. I remember when I was a little barefoot girl, the day came to wear my first pair of shoes. The shoes protected my feet, but also separated me from the touch of the grass. In the same way, the roof divides us from the stars."

"Oriana," said Arthur, "I never would want these machines to divide me from you."

The next morning, before sunrise, Arthur wandered to the sauropod barn. He found Will, who had just finished some early chores. They had an opportunity to talk privately for the first time in a long while. Arthur told Will the entire tale of the

journey through the World Beneath and then showed him the statuette of Ogthar.

Will was excited. "So that's King Ogthar? I think I found the ruins of his jungle palace. There were carvings everywhere of him and *Tyrannosaurus rex.*"

Arthur sat up straight. "Rex," he said. "That's it! The word 'rex' means king. The old scrolls told of the treasure being under a new king's protection. Well, that king is *Tyrannosaurus rex.* That's why we were being attacked. Somewhere in that Palace of Kings must be the lost treasure of Poseidos."

Will whispered, "What if Crabb finds out?"

Thick vegetation shields them from attack, but slows progress

CRABB MUST ALREADY HAVE SOLVED the mystery of the treasure, for he had slipped away unnoticed on his strutter during the breakfast hour. Arthur's sketchbook, which was kept wrapped in waterproof oilskin, was missing as well. The bridgekeeper said he had seen something far away scaling the cliffs and crossing the Polongo River toward the Rainy Basin.

Arthur, Oriana, and Bix decided to follow in their own strutter, knowing they had sufficient speed to outrun any pursuers. Will and Sylvia flew a decoy mission along the main convoy route, while the strutter stayed off the trail to hide from the theropods. The undergrowth was so choked with *Angiopteris* and other gigantic ferns that they could see very little ahead of them. When they neared the ruins of the Palace of Kings, they tiptoed the strutter through weed-infested canals.

Eventually they had to leave the strutter and continue on foot. Oriana heard the noise of thrashing and growling. Peering over the wall of vegetation, she whispered, "Come look. Two meat-eaters. I think they're playing."

Two juvenile theropods
wrestle playfully

Standtall

Fireblood

Arthur frees
Standtall's foot

The two dinosaurs tackled each other and
rolled on the soft mat of leaves. "Those are
juveniles," said Bix. "See, they are playful, like
all young hunters."

"But they're not tyrannosaurs, are they, Bix?"
asked Oriana.

"Not with three fingers on their hands."

Just then the dinosaurs jumped onto a log-
jam of fallen trees. One of them slipped and
trapped his foot in a tangle of logs.

Bix exchanged hoots and calls with the creature and then turned to Arthur. "He won't
hurt you. He wants you to pull his foot free."

[130]

Enchanted by the dragon flute

The young hunters studied Oriana and Bix with immense curiosity, as if they were seeing a human and a *Protoceratops* for the first time. Oriana brought out her dragon flute and began to weave a melody so enchanting that the dinosaurs stood spellbound.

Bix spoke to them in surprisingly low, harsh tones. She then translated the response. "He thanks you, Arthur, for getting him out of a jam. His name is Standtall, and he is a *Giganotosaurus*, which means 'giant from the south.' He says he wants us to meet his father, Stinktooth."

Arthur pulled at his collar. "I don't like the sound of this," he said.

"We don't have much choice but to go along," said Bix. "But don't worry. Bloodthirsty as they seem to outsiders, these creatures can be fiercely loyal, and they have a powerful sense of honor and justice. Because of your act of kindness, I believe we have just earned merit."

[131]

They came to the edge of a clearing. All at once a tyrannosaur turned to face them. But just as it did, an even bigger meat-eater, the largest Bix had ever seen, loomed above their heads.

He let out a ground-rattling roar so terrifying that the trees swayed, and the tyrannosaur cowered in submission.

"That's the father," said Bix, "and he's protecting us."

Copperjaw, a Tyrannosaurus rex

Skull length: 154 cm
Femur length: 138 cm
Overall length: 14 m

Two fingers

Stinktooth, a
Giganotosaurus

Skull length: 157cm
Femur length: 143 cm
Overall length: 15 m

Three fingers

No one dares comment on Stinktooth's bad breath

Cryolophosaurus

Carnotaurus

"Amazing!" Arthur whispered to Oriana. "He's larger than *Tyrannosaurus rex*."

"That makes him the king of kings," Oriana replied.

"The king of halitosis," groaned Bix.

Mercifully the giant kept his mouth closed, watching over them in brooding silence. To the other theropods around him, Stinktooth remained unquestionably in command. One by one he permitted the smaller meat-eaters to investigate the newcomers. Arthur did not enjoy the feeling of scaly muzzles rubbing against him, even though Bix insisted that it was meant as a gesture of acceptance.

[135]

An assembly of titans gathered in the heavy mist that shrouded the ruins. Stinktooth presided at the center of all, cool and unshakable.

"What should we do?" Arthur asked Bix nervously.

"He knows we're interested in the treasure," she answered. "I think we should let him know we don't want to steal anything."

Arthur reached into his pocket for the small statuette of Ogthar. He placed it on the rock before the *Giganotosaurus*.

Oriana joined him and laid down her dragon flute. Then, glancing at each other, Arthur and Oriana set down the two halves of the key. They returned to where Bix was standing.

Stinktooth gave a single, low growl.

"He says to keep your treasures," translated Bix. "You are worthy. But remember to take only what you can hold in your mind."

Face to face with the king of kings

[136]

Doorway beneath the giant strangler fig

They passed through an elemental wilderness of root and stone. Slowly, inexorably, the trees struggled against the ruins, as if determined to scatter them to dust and chaos.

Well-hidden beneath the roots of an immense fig tree was a doorway. They stepped inside, adjusting their eyes to the gloom, exploring deeper into a maze of mossy hallways. Then they saw it: dazzling and glowing, the fruit of a thousand royal workshops, a small sea of riches adorning the feet of a gigantic statue of Ogthar.

"What Crabb would give for this," murmured Arthur.

Plaque near the door of the treasure room tells the legend of the ruby sunstone

Gold bust of Almestra, a Chandaran queen who married a king of Poseidos

The treasure of Poseidos surpassed their wildest imaginings. There were gems beyond reckoning, untarnished metals of lustrous hues, craftsmanship of the finest skill and delicacy, and scientific instruments of forgotten purpose.

Oriana stopped to run her fingers over a gold portrait statue. "I have found her," she said softly, thinking of her vision in the caves. "A queen."

Arthur, who had been standing nearby, put his arm around her waist and kissed her cheek. "She's not half the queen that I've discovered."

Bix trotted over and peered at the statue. "Chandaran," she chirped. "Fifth Kingdom."

Arthur, trying to overcome his irritation at Bix's untimely entrance, said, "You mean this isn't Egyptian?"

"Of course not. Thousands of years ago, a group of Chandarans managed to travel off-island and export a bit of their civilization."

"Egypt was influenced by Dinotopians?"

"Yes, of course," said Bix. "And the motif of the Chinese dragon traces back to early sightings of dinosaurs here."

"There's something else," said Arthur. "Atlantis."

"What is Atlantis?" asked Oriana.

"The outer world has a myth much like your story of Poseidos. They must be one and the same. After all, according to Plato, Atlantis belonged to Poseidon, lord of the sea."

"Poseidos…Poseidon…" said Bix. "Reports have a way of being garbled as they are passed down."

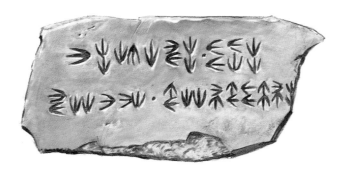

A warning

Arthur continued exploring and made a startling discovery: a photographic device that must have been older than the pyramids. Near it was a polished wooden box filled with stacks of elliptical silver plate exposures. "These are daguerreotypes! Absolute proof that the lost city of Poseidos existed."

An ancient camera

Music box in the form of a Lambeosaurus

Poseidos in its glory

Arthur studied images of markets, busy streets, and festivals. Oriana found other exposures with a more haunting vision: flooded harbors, drowning monuments, and struggling survivors. The pictures told the entire story. Architects with a grand vision established the capital of their mechanized empire on an island in Sapphire Bay, little knowing that the foundations of the city were weakened by the empty volcanic caverns that lay below. The people of Poseidos squandered their divine gifts and grew enslaved to the very machines they built as servants. Most of the dinosaurs, no longer needed, left the city. Then, during the crowning days of the empire, a single ruby sunstone was found in the mines. This stone had the power to magnify dark desires in anything it touched, human or machine. When the city began to settle into its hollow base, the waters poured into the streets. Most of the survivors fled to Prosperine. The ruby sunstone was rescued by the king and his followers, along with the royal treasury and a small fleet of strutters, and was carried into hiding along the underground barge canal. They lived below ground as long as they could, trying to rebuild their laboratories in the caverns. But eventually, divided by strife, they emerged from the caves in search of a new life. The cursed treasure was given over to the tyrannosaurs as the price of safe passage through the Rainy Basin, and there it has stayed to this day.

A voice stirred the silence in the next room. "Pretty trinkets, eh, Professor?"

Escaping the drowning city

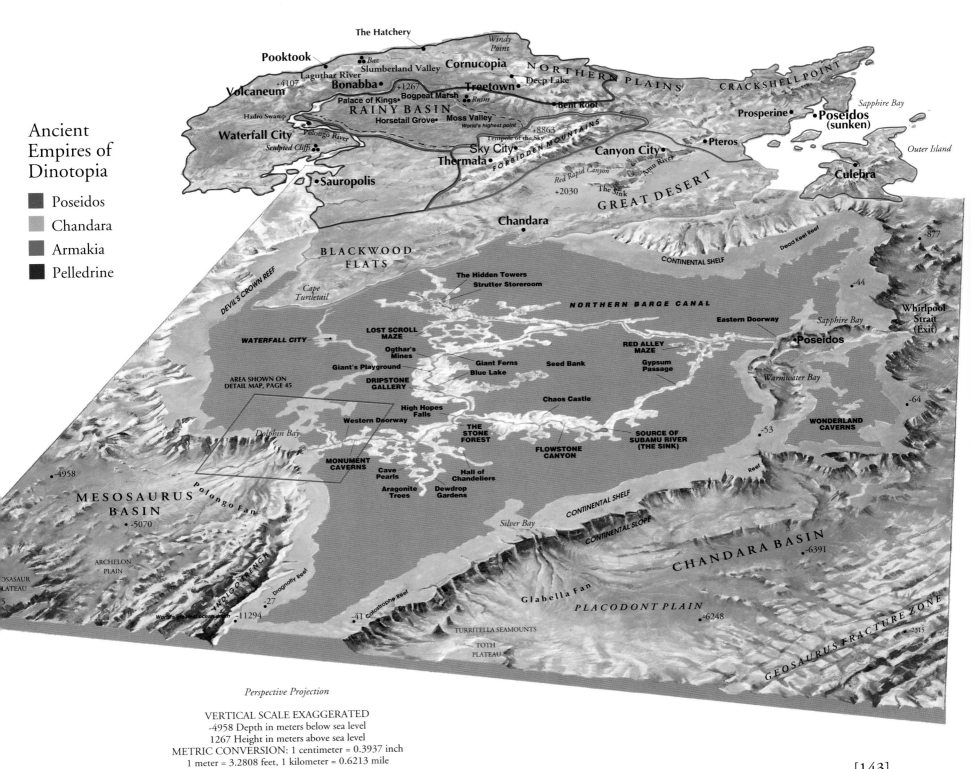

The caverns and the ocean floor beneath Dinotopia

Ancient Empires of Dinotopia

- Poseidos
- Chandara
- Armakia
- Pelledrine

The Hatchery

Pooktook

Windy Point

Baz
Slumberland Valley **Cornucopia**

Laguthar River **NORTHERN PLAINS** CRACKSHELL POINT

Volcaneum +4107 **Bonabba** +1267 **Treetown** Deep Lake

Palace of Kings Bogpeat Marsh *Ruins* Bent Root

Hadro Swamp **RAINY BASIN** Horsetail Grove Moss Valley *Sapphire Bay*

Waterfall City *Polongo River* *World's highest point* **Prosperine** **Poseidos** (sunken)

Sculpted Cliffs Tentpole of the Sky +8863 **FORBIDDEN MOUNTAINS** *Outer Island*

Sky City **Pteros**

Thermala **Canyon City**

Sauropolis +2030 *Red Rapid Canyon* *Amu River* **Culebra**

The Sink **GREAT DESERT**

Chandara

-877

BLACKWOOD FLATS *Dead Keel Reef*

CONTINENTAL SHELF

DEVIL'S CROWN REEF *Cape Turtletail* The Hidden Towers Strutter Storeroom **NORTHERN BARGE CANAL** -44

Eastern Doorway *Sapphire Bay* Whirlpool Strait (Exit)

WATERFALL CITY **LOST SCROLL MAZE**

Ogthar's Mines **RED ALLEY MAZE** **Poseidos**

Giant's Playground Giant Ferns Seed Bank Gypsum Passage

DRIPSTONE GALLERY Blue Lake *Warmwater Bay*

AREA SHOWN ON DETAIL MAP, PAGE 45 Chaos Castle

High Hopes Falls

Western Doorway **THE STONE FOREST** SOURCE OF SUBAMU RIVER (THE SINK) **WONDERLAND CAVERNS**

Dolphin Bay -53

-64

MONUMENT CAVERNS Cave Pearls FLOWSTONE CANYON *Reef*

-4958 Aragonite Trees Hall of Chandeliers CONTINENTAL SHELF

Dewdrop Gardens

MESOSAURUS BASIN *Polongo Fan* *Silver Bay* CONTINENTAL SLOPE

-5070

CHANDARA BASIN -6391

ARCHELON PLAIN *Glabella Fan*

OSASAUR PLATEAU *Dragonfly Reef* INDIGO TRENCH -27 *Catastrophe Reef* -41 **PLACODONT PLAIN** -6248

5 *World's greatest ocean depth* -11294 TURRITELLA SEAMOUNTS **GEOSAURUS FRACTURE ZONE**

TOTH PLATEAU -2315

Perspective Projection

VERTICAL SCALE EXAGGERATED
-4958 Depth in meters below sea level
1267 Height in meters above sea level
METRIC CONVERSION: 1 centimeter = 0.3937 inch
1 meter = 3.2808 feet, 1 kilometer = 0.6213 mile

Lee Crabb steals
the ruby sunstone

Arthur's strutter is destroyed

"LISTEN, CAPTAIN. I'LL MAKE IT SWEET," said Crabb. "I've got a strutter full of loot; I've got the red rock here; I've got all of your notes; and I know from the maps how to get off this island. Here's my bargain. You and I ship out together, and we find a buyer for all this fancy science. We split the profits fifty-fifty, and then we build a fleet of attack strutters. The world would be ours, and we could come back and rid this island of scalies."

"No," said Arthur. "I don't want your profits and I don't want your attack strutters. I won't let you go."

"All right, Denison," said Crabb contemptuously. "Stay with the skinnies and scalies, if you please. But try to stop me and I'll make shark food out of you."

In an instant Crabb scurried through a concealed tunnel to where his strutter was hidden. He clamped the ruby sunstone in his machine and destroyed Arthur's strutter with terrible force. By the time Stinktooth arrived, Crabb was already lost to sight. Quickly grasping the situation, Stinktooth lowered his head and let Arthur climb onto his shoulders.

It was a chase not soon to be
forgotten. The tyrannosaurs could not
stop Crabb inside the Rainy Basin. Even
Stinktooth and his mate, who were allowed across
the bridge, could not halt the furious march of
Crabb's strutter to the sea. Will, flying high above,
called to Sylvia, "Go up to Prosperine and get some
northies! We'll need help."

Stinktooth can swim no farther

Crabb ignores Arthur's pleas to stop

Crabb's strutter tore into the surf, the ruby sunstone glowing with an ominous light. Stinktooth followed with all his force, but he was built for land, and the rolling canyons of salt water nearly drowned him.

As if by instinct, Arthur jumped free and fought his way onto the back of the strutter. He struggled to hold on, even as the strutter ducked under the waves. Arthur pounded on the window and shouted for Crabb to stop. Ignoring him, Crabb just chewed his cigar defiantly and squeezed the power trigger.

Casting away the ruby sunstone

There was nothing Arthur could do but unclamp the ruby sunstone. With his bare hands numbed by the icy water, and fighting the sharp shocks of the sunstone's defensive field, he pulled it loose from the bracket and hurled it as far as he could. It shimmered down into the darkness beneath the waves.

The strutter groaned and sank deeper in the water. Arthur pried open the cockpit, and pulled Crabb out by the collar.

Will and Sylvia spotted them on the sinking strutter. Alongside the skybax riders flew two *Quetzalcoatlus northropi* wearing rescue harnesses. Northies were strong, steady fliers, but not accustomed to riders on their backs. They swooped low, just in time to hoist Arthur and Crabb up into the sky.

The rescue of Lee Crabb and Arthur Denison

The lost city reclaims its prizes

Unknown to all of them, the ruins of Poseidos lay on the sea floor directly below them. The ruby sunstone settled quietly into the sand, followed not long after by the derelict strutter.

One object alone escaped with a last rush of bubbles. It was a small package, wrapped tightly in oilskin. It bobbed up to the surface of Sapphire Bay and drifted northeast through Whirlpool Strait and into the wide ocean. A Philippine fisherman named Diego Ramón discovered the package seven months later near Cape San Ildefonso. The object sealed inside was a leather-bound sketchbook containing drawings, scientific diagrams, and pressed botanical specimens.

Thus began the sketchbook's even longer journey through a chain of collectors and curiosity dealers until it came to rest where it now resides, in the University Library.

Arthur's sketchbook is discovered

A son and his father

Will and Arthur stood together high on a bluff above the sea. "I think my sketchbook is gone for good," Arthur said.

"Let's hope it *is* for good," Will replied. "Whoever finds it will know a lot more about this island."

"They probably won't believe it," reflected Arthur. "And if they do, well, better knowledge than ignorance." He took a deep breath.

"But better still is wisdom," he continued. "And I suppose I've had that in short supply lately."

"Oriana says you need to talk to more dinosaurs," said Will, laughing.

Crabb had lost a little of his swagger, but none of his salt. He was placed under the watch of two spike-headed wardens, who followed his every movement both day and night. Stinktooth and his mate received honors gracefully but were glad to return to the Rainy Basin, where they felt at home.

Crabb is watched by a pair of Stygimoloch

Gruff

Duff

Nallab, assistant librarian

Bix tells her story

Enit

Malik

Bix returned to the comforts she had gone so long without, just as happy to tell her tale as the librarians were to record it, so that future ages could hear it told many times again.

In puppet shows and in songs, in dances and in dreams, the legend of the Denison Expedition lived on in the hearts of children and hatchlings, who grew more eager each day for their own adventures.

[156]

And what do the old scrolls say about Arthur and Oriana? Only that their lives grew to intertwine as did the two halves of their key, which they kept intact beside the hearth. They discovered in Waterfall City, and in each other, a grandeur that nourished them from the mists of the morning to the last light of the fading day.

The soft blanket of twilight comforts the sleepy world